☆☆☆ ARLO & PIPS ☆☆☆

KING OF THE BIRDS

ELISE GRAVEL

HARPER
alley

An Imprint of HarperCollinsPublishers

HarperAlley is an imprint of HarperCollins Publishers.

Arlo & Pips: King of the Birds
Copyright © 2020 by Elise Gravel
All rights reserved. Manufactured in Slovenia.
No part of this book may be used or reproduced in any manner whatsoever without written permission except in the case
of brief quotations embodied in critical articles and reviews. For information address HarperCollins Children's Books, a
division of HarperCollins Publishers, 195 Broadway, New York, NY 10007.

www.harpercollinschildrens.com

ISBN 978-0-06-298221-6 (tr.) — 978-0-06-298222-3 (pbk.)

The artist used Photoshop to create the digital illustrations for this book.
Typography by Elise Gravel and Chrisila Maida
20 21 22 23 24 GPS 10 9 8 7 6 5 4 3 2 1

❖
First Edition

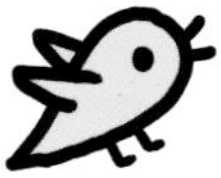

For Enzo,
who is almost an Arlo

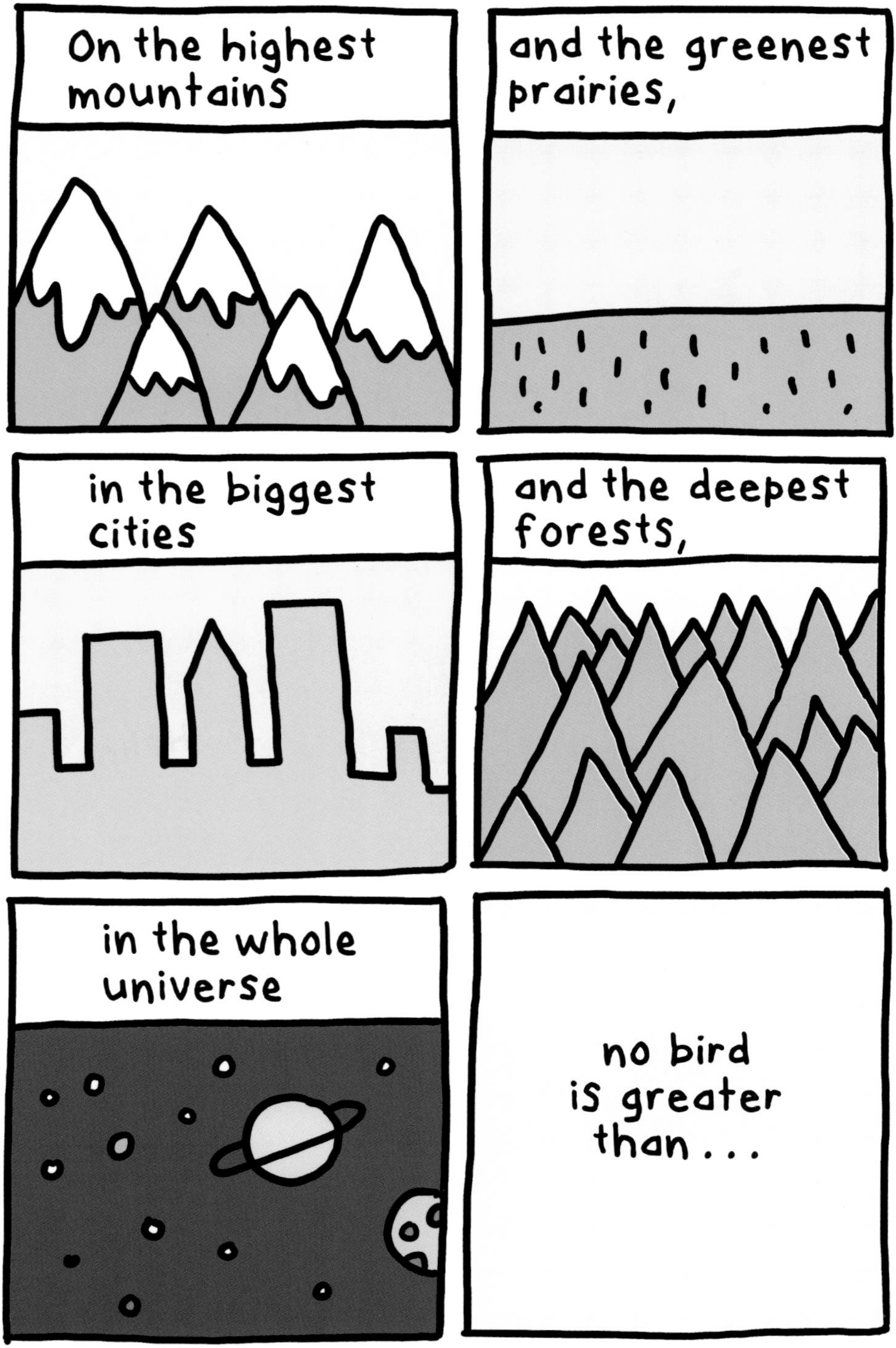
On the highest mountains
and the greenest prairies,
in the biggest cities
and the deepest forests,
in the whole universe
no bird is greater than . . .

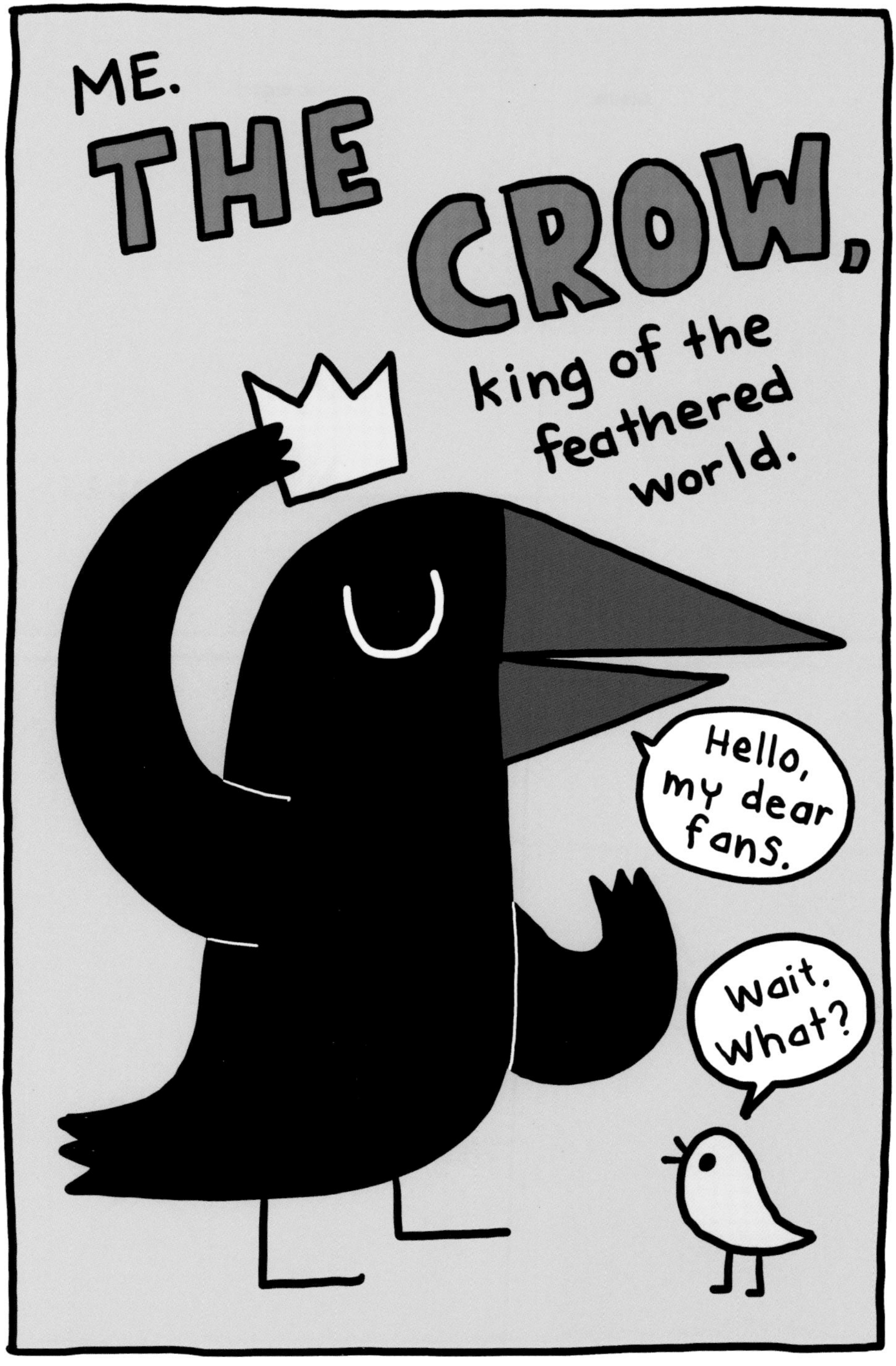
ME.
THE CROW,
king of the feathered world.
Hello, my dear fans.
Wait. What?

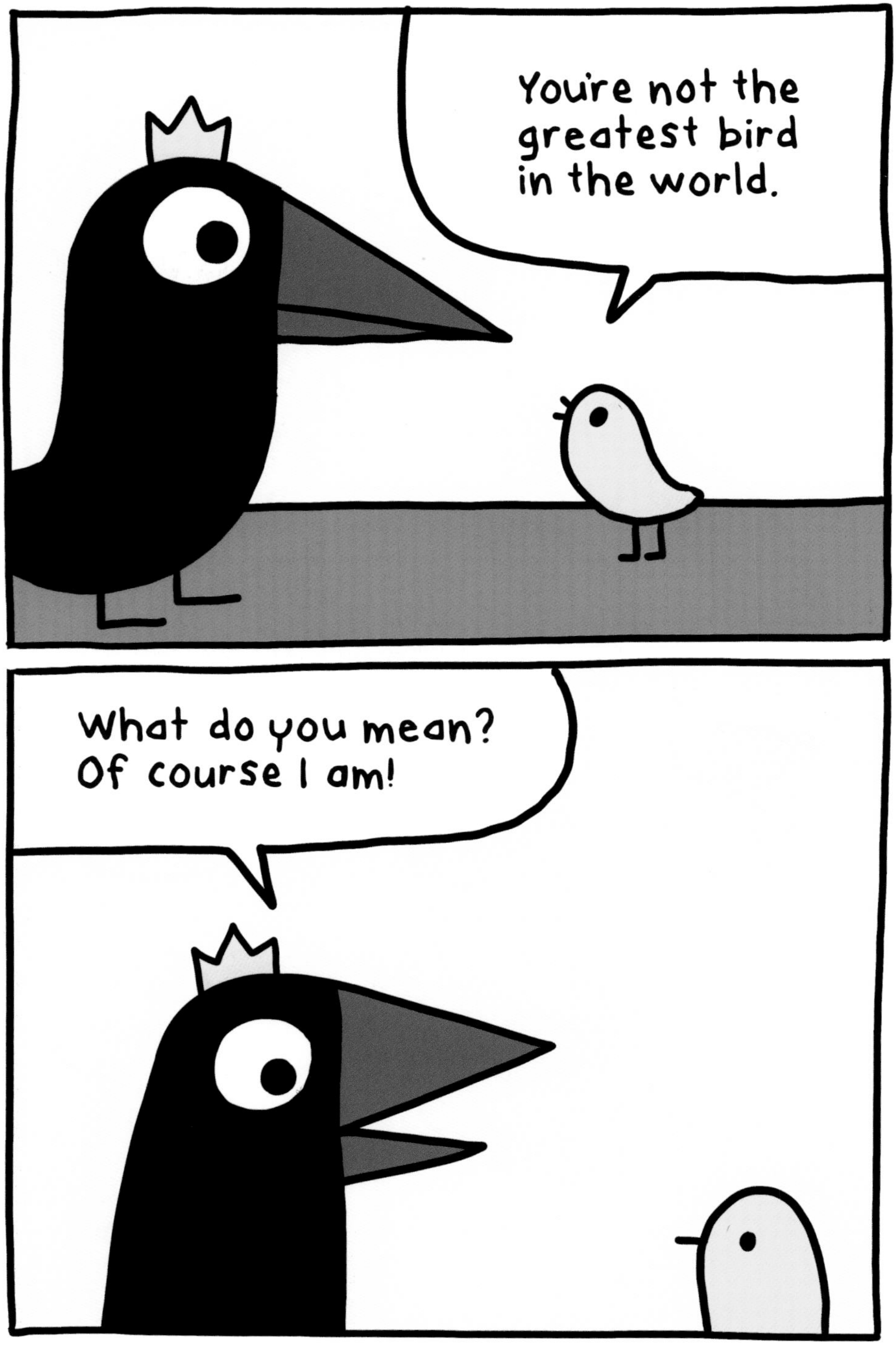
You're not the greatest bird in the world.
What do you mean? Of course I am!

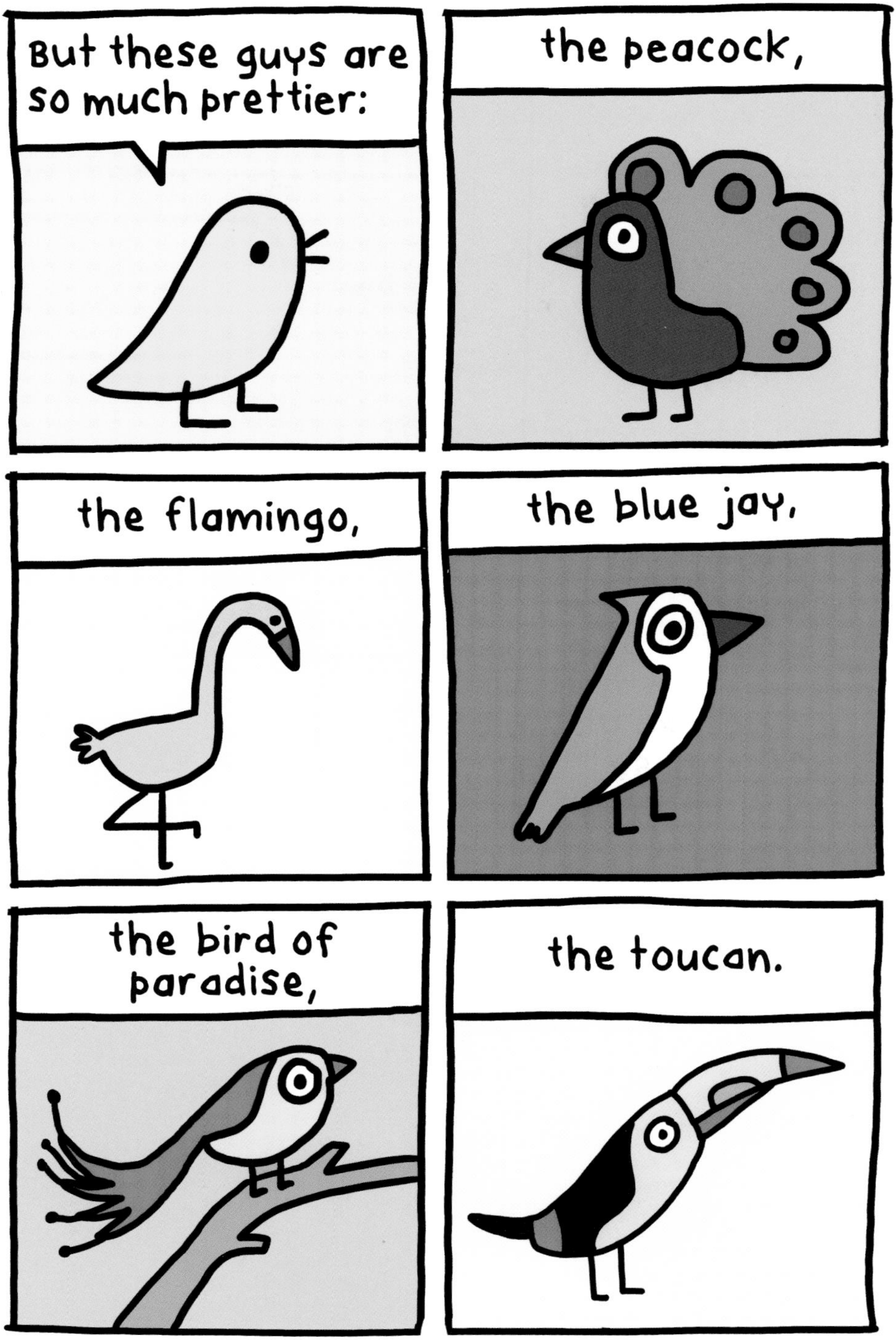
But these guys are so much prettier:
the peacock,
the flamingo,
the blue jay,
the bird of paradise,
the toucan.

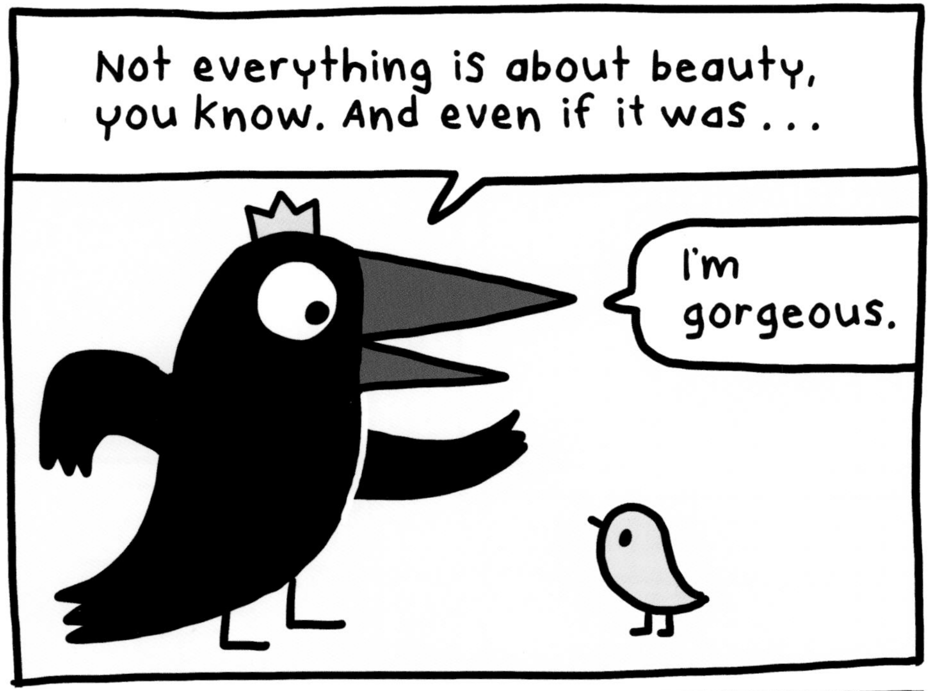
Not everything is about beauty, you know. And even if it was . . .
I'm gorgeous.

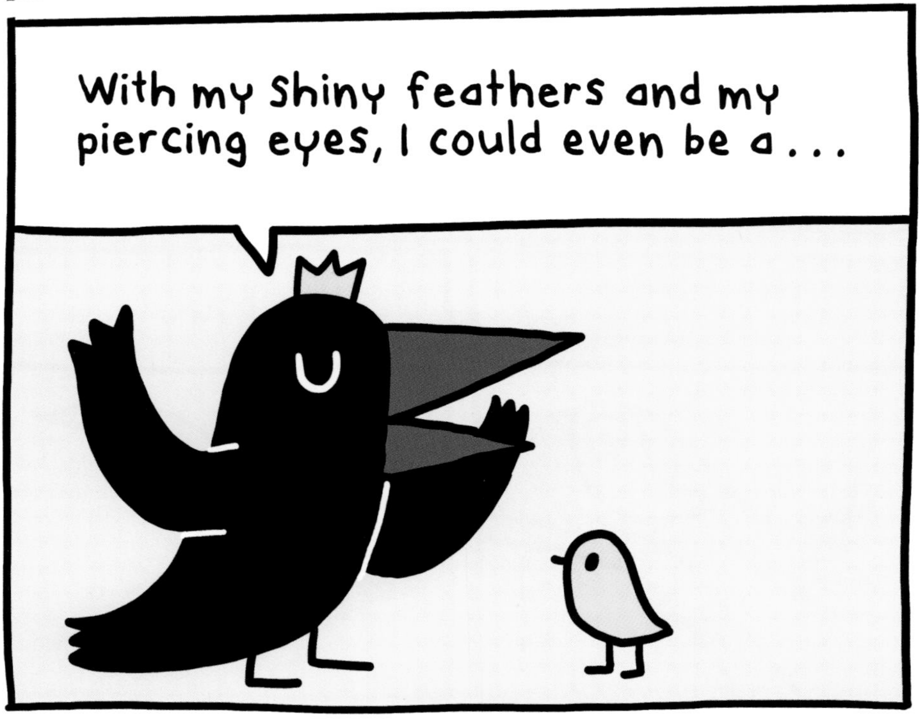
With my shiny feathers and my piercing eyes, I could even be a . . .

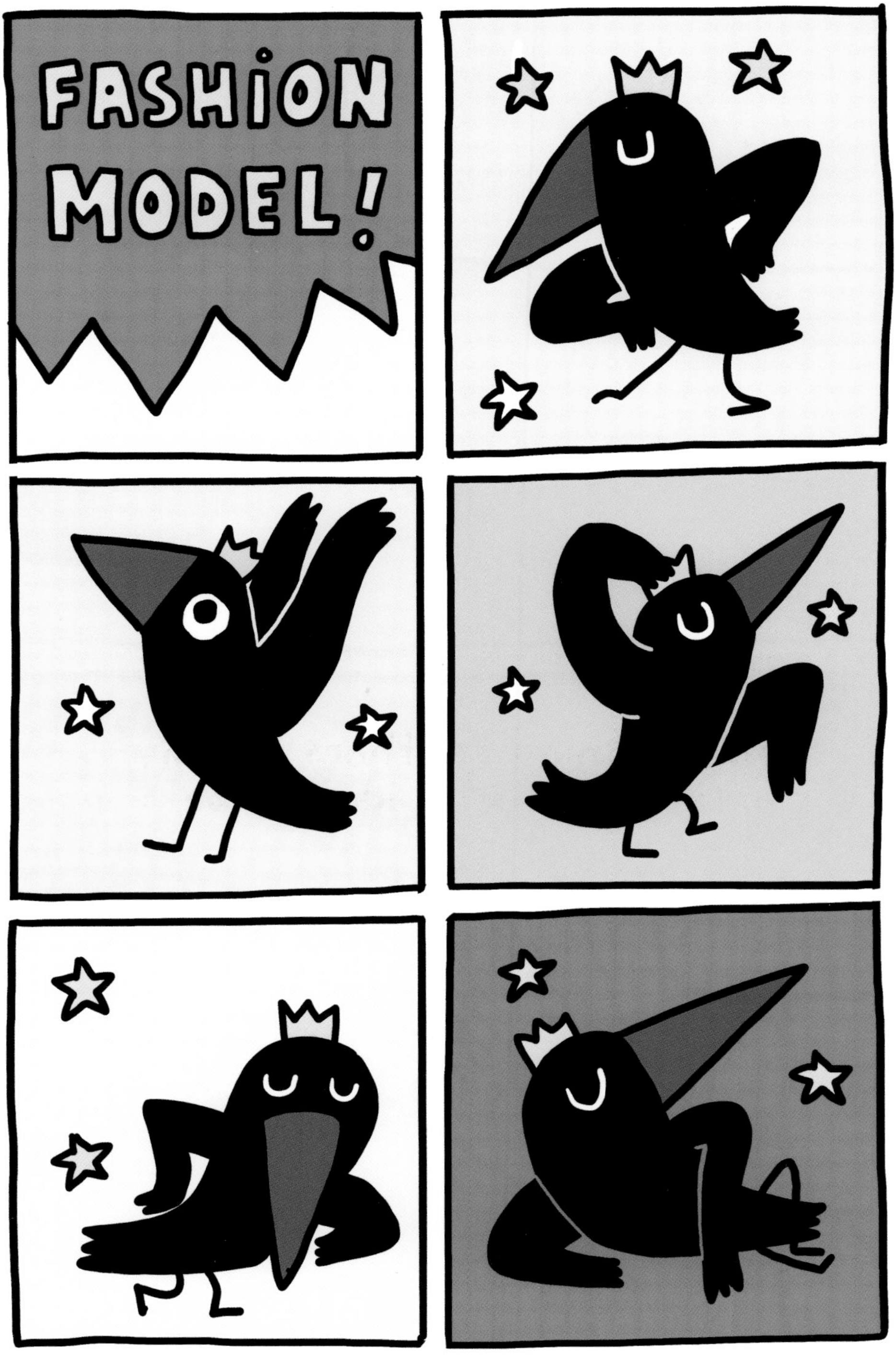
FASHION MODEL!

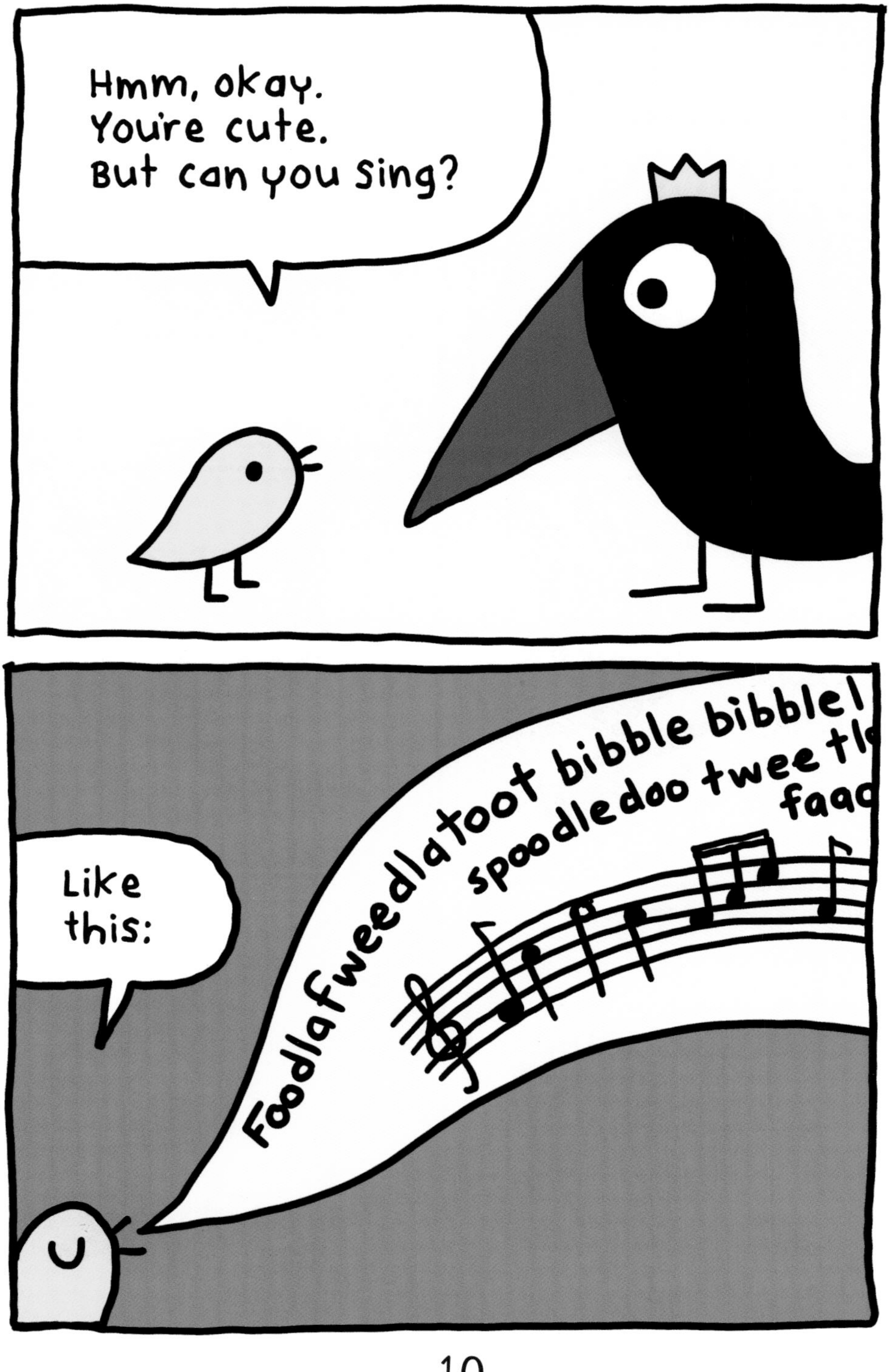
Hmm, okay.
You're cute.
But can you sing?
Like this:
Foodlafweedlatoot bibble bibblel
spoodledoo tweetl
faa

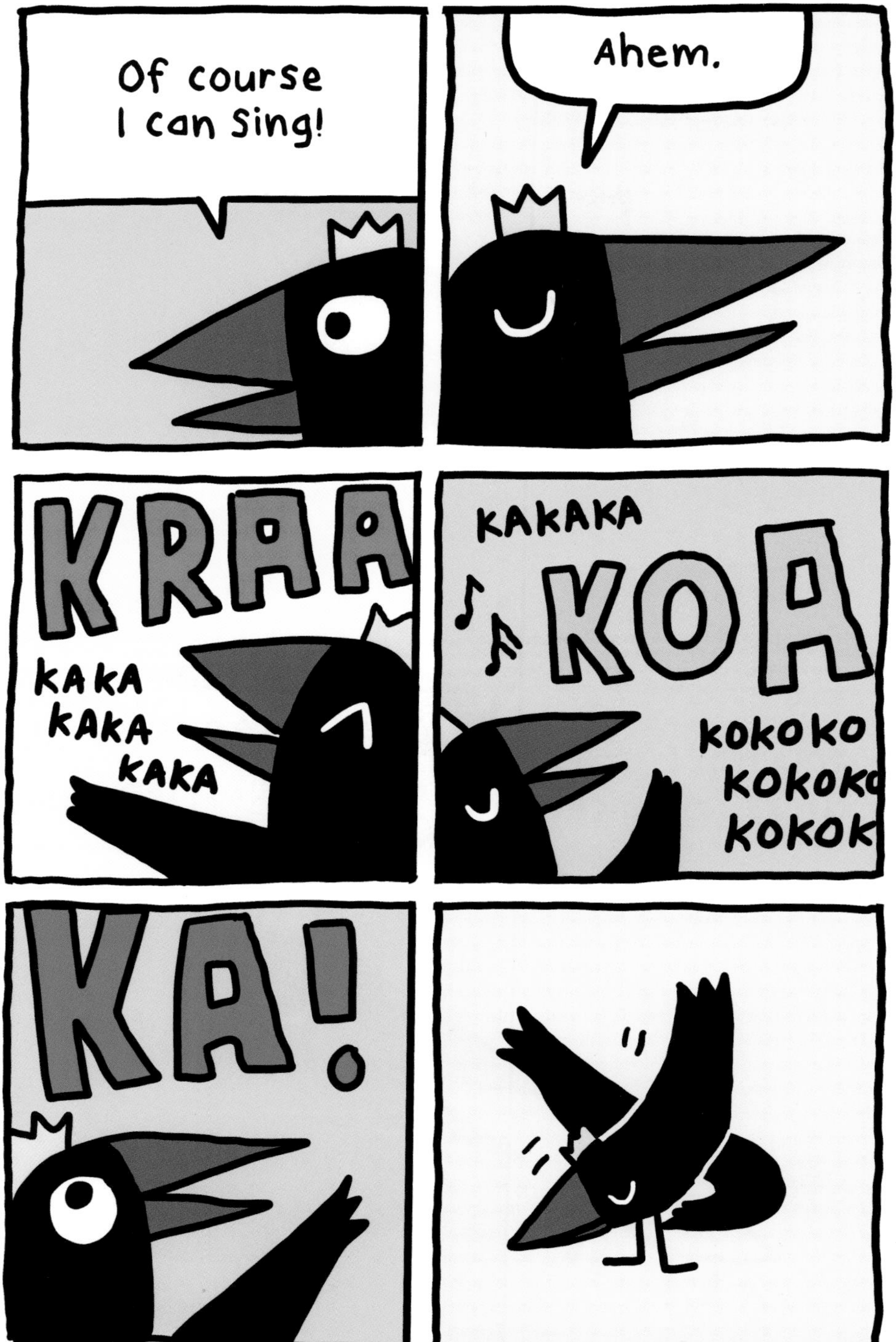
Of course I can sing!
Ahem.
KRAA
KAKA KAKA KAKA
KAKAKA
KOA
KOKOKO KOKOKO KOKOK
KA!

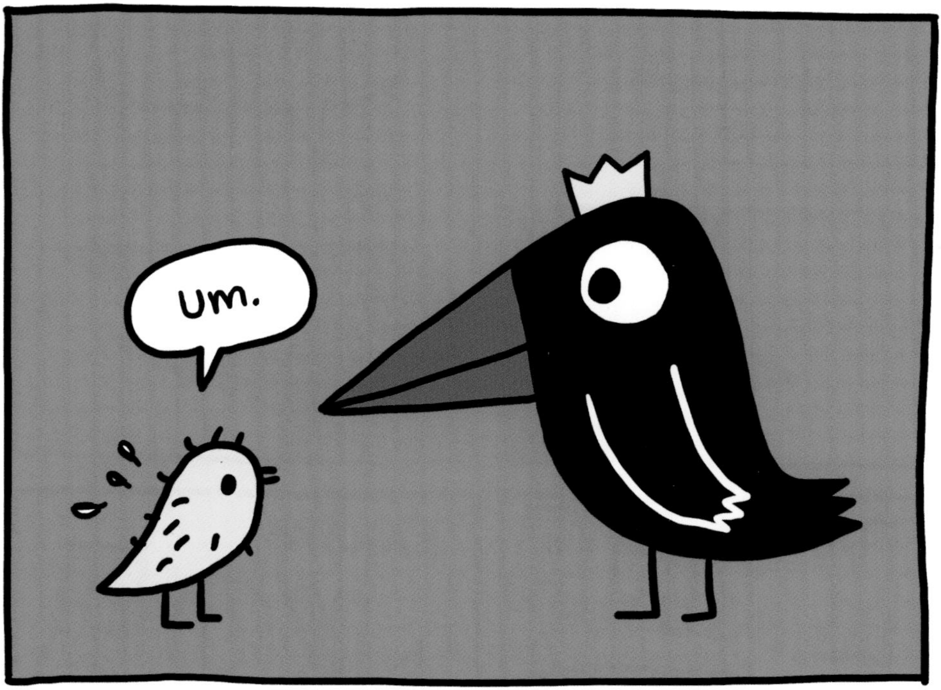
Um.

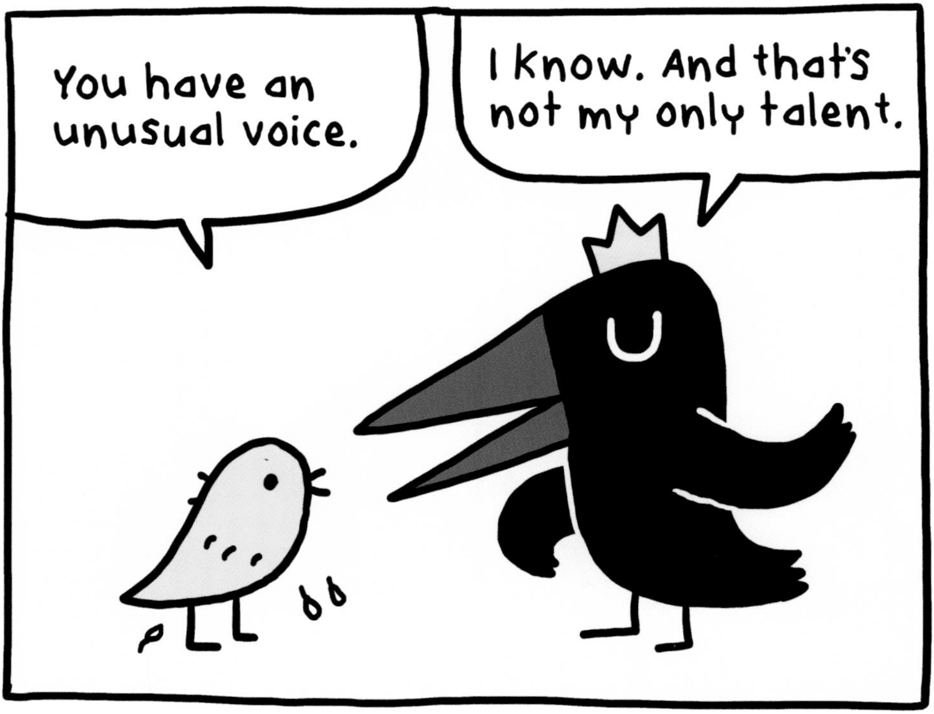
You have an unusual voice.
I know. And that's not my only talent.

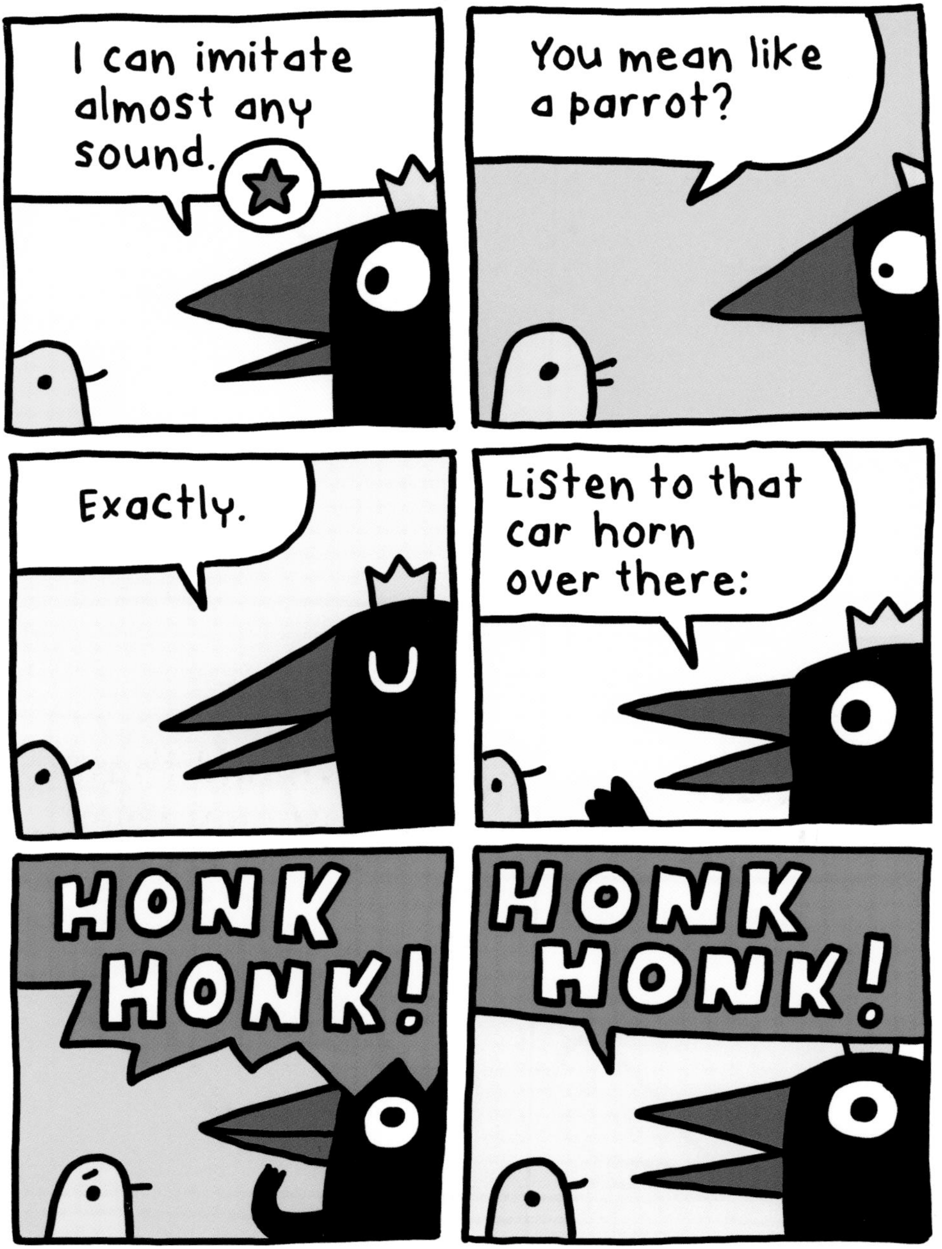
I can imitate almost any sound.
You mean like a parrot?
Exactly.
Listen to that car horn over there:
HONK HONK!
HONK HONK!

★ Crows are very good at imitating sounds, including human voices and words.

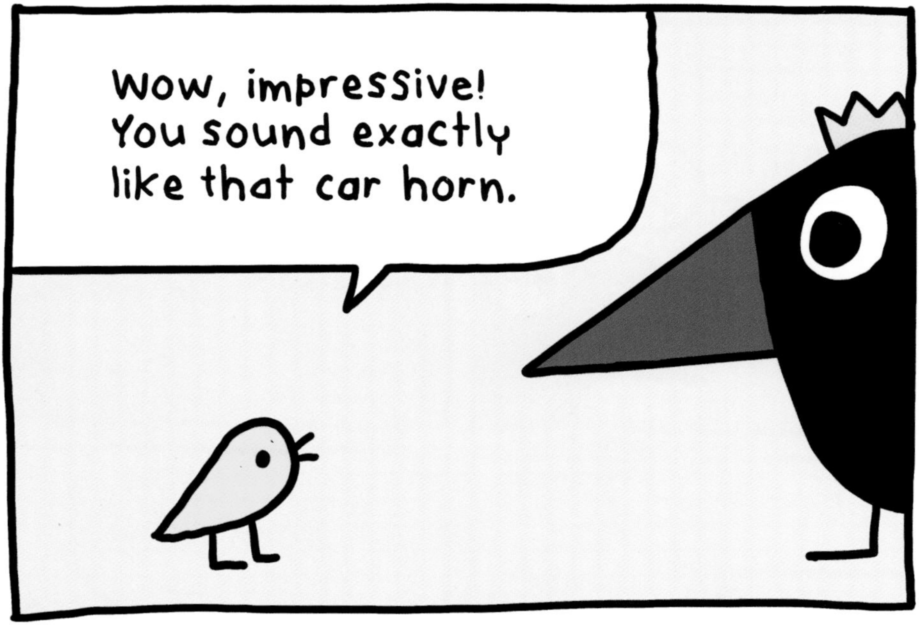
Wow, impressive! You sound exactly like that car horn.

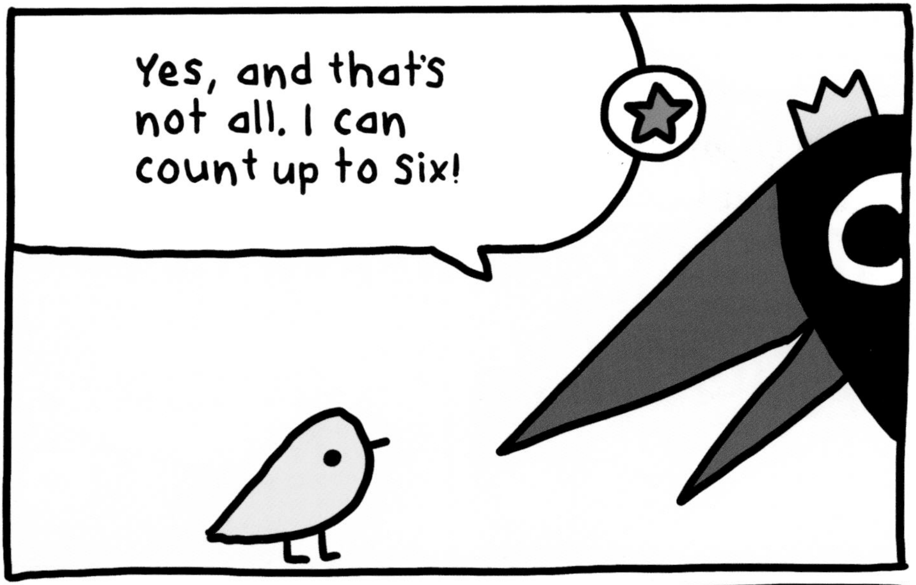
Yes, and that's not all. I can count up to six!

Crows can count up to six objects, maybe more. They might even be able to add!

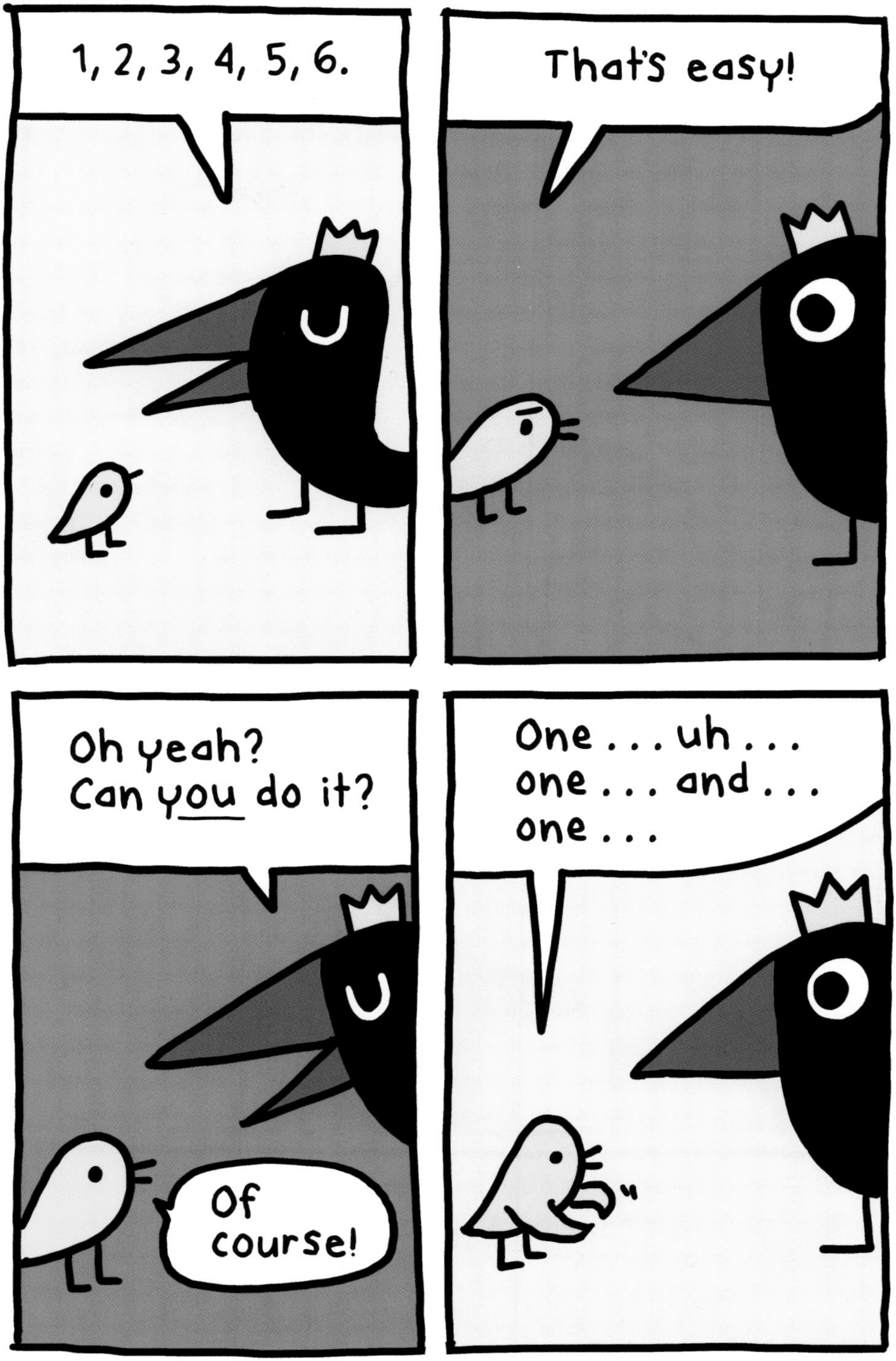
1, 2, 3, 4, 5, 6.
That's easy!
Oh yeah?
Can you do it?
Of course!
One . . . uh . . .
one . . . and . . .
one . . .

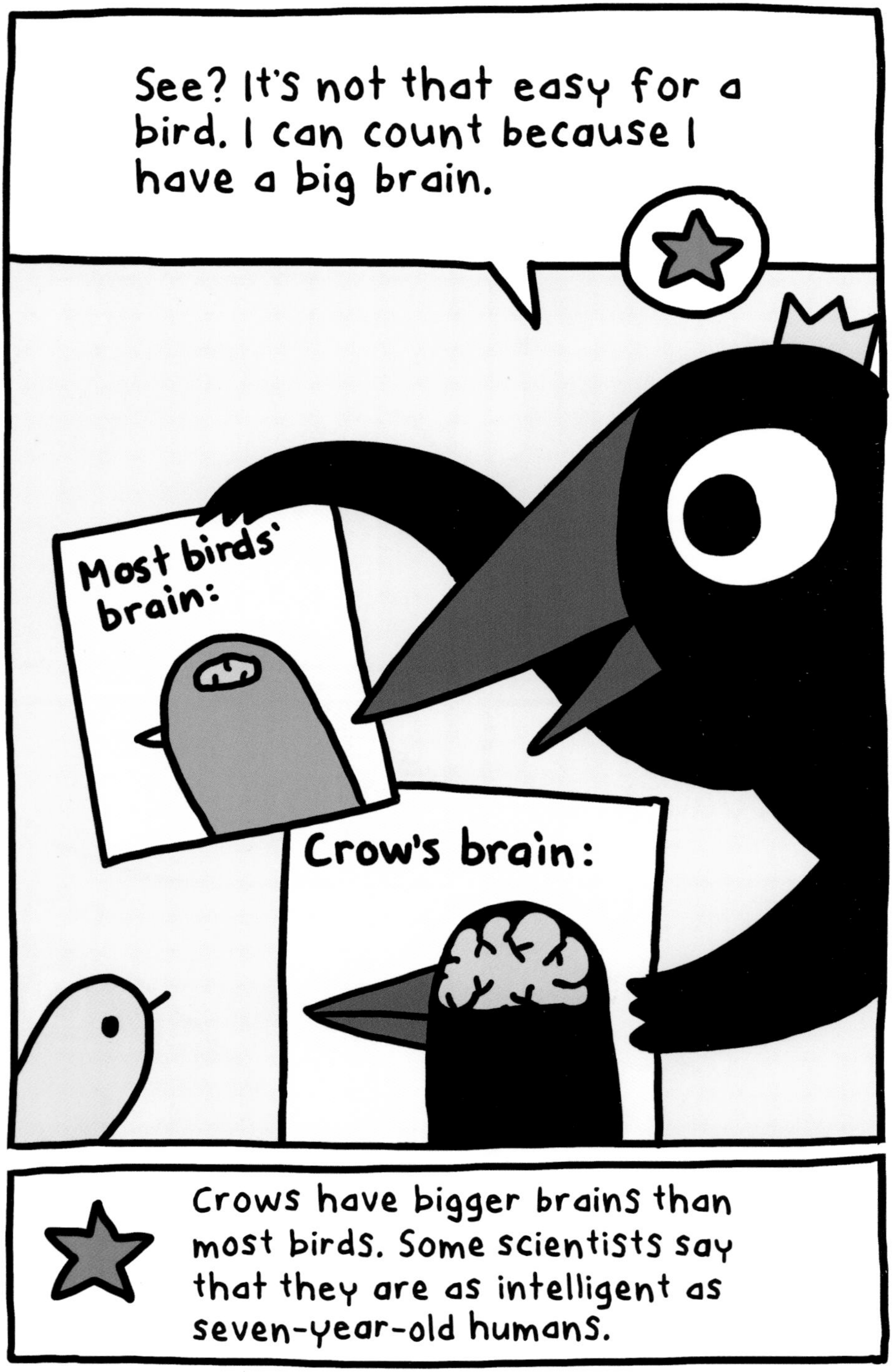
See? It's not that easy for a bird. I can count because I have a big brain.
Most birds' brain:
Crow's brain:
Crows have bigger brains than most birds. Some scientists say that they are as intelligent as seven-year-old humans.

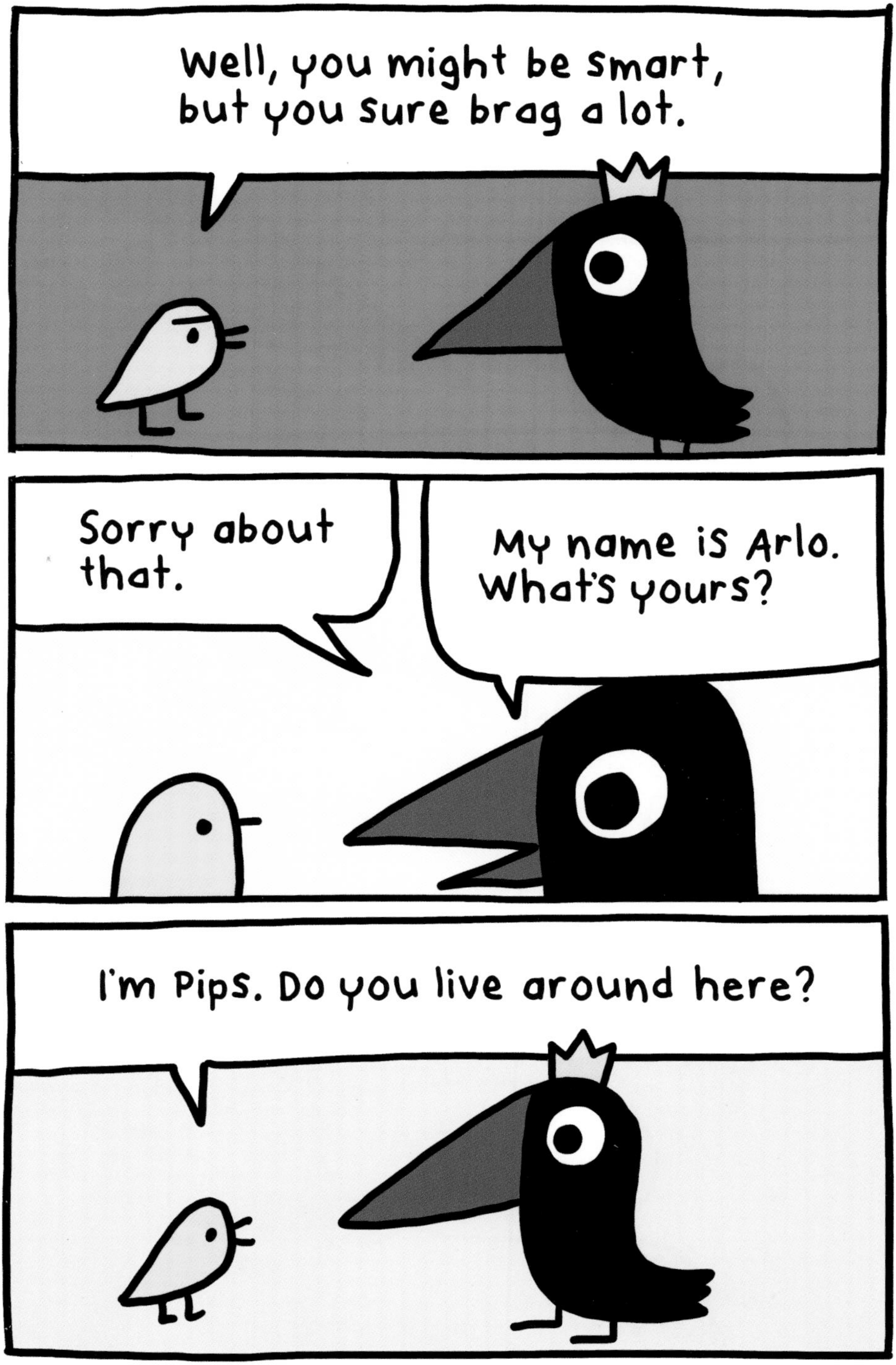
Well, you might be smart, but you sure brag a lot.
Sorry about that.
My name is Arlo. What's yours?
I'm Pips. Do you live around here?

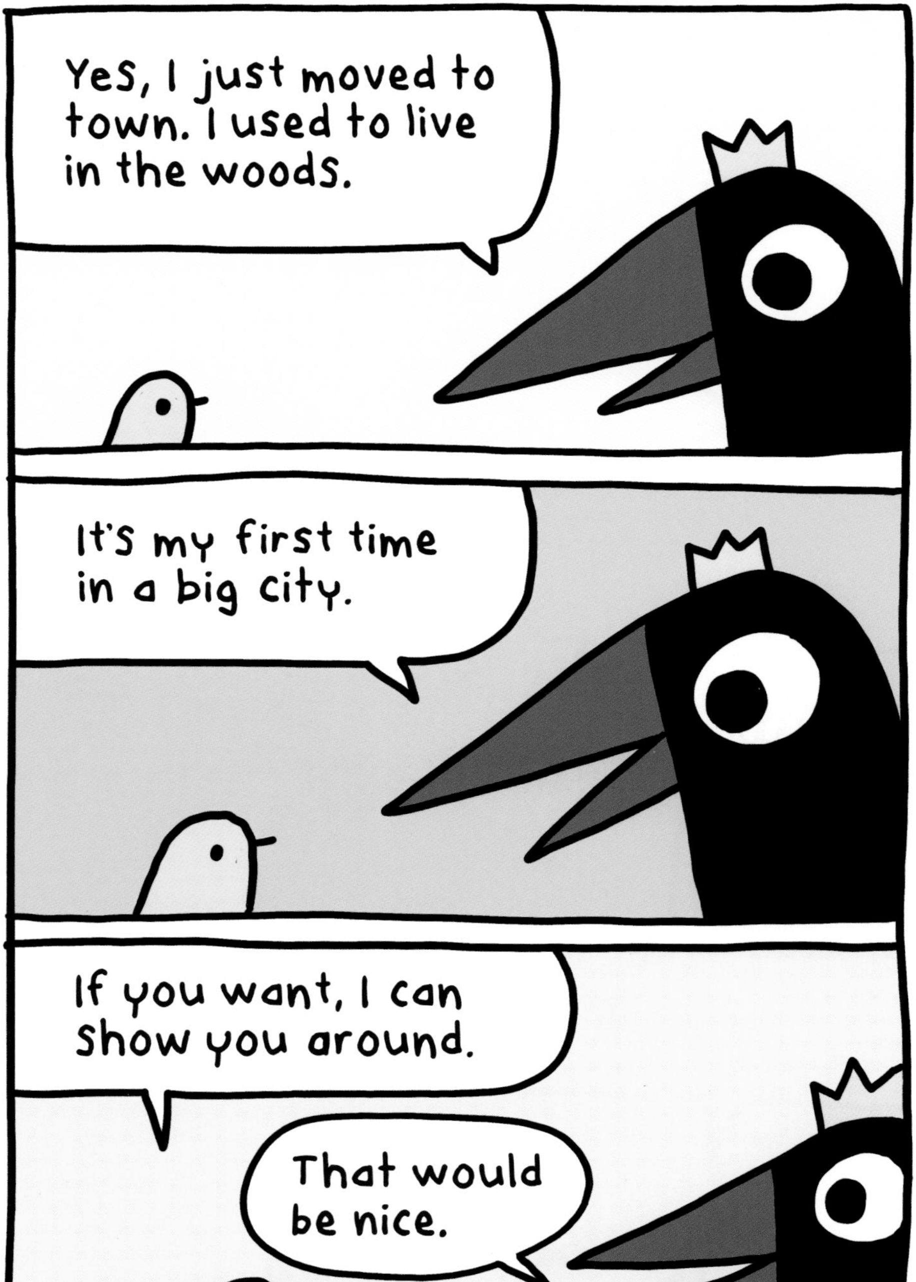
Yes, I just moved to town. I used to live in the woods.
It's my first time in a big city.
If you want, I can show you around.
That would be nice.

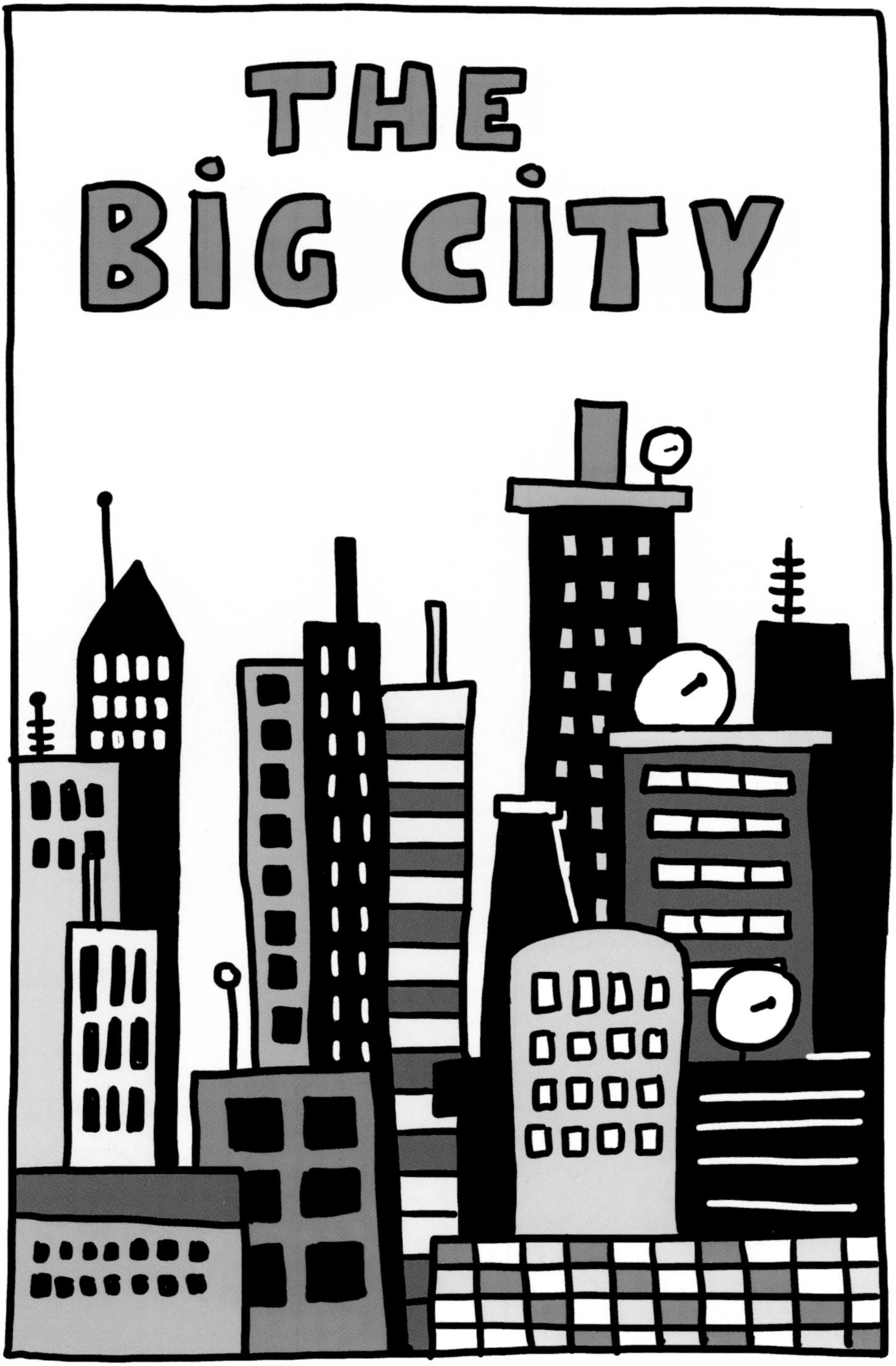
THE
BIG CITY

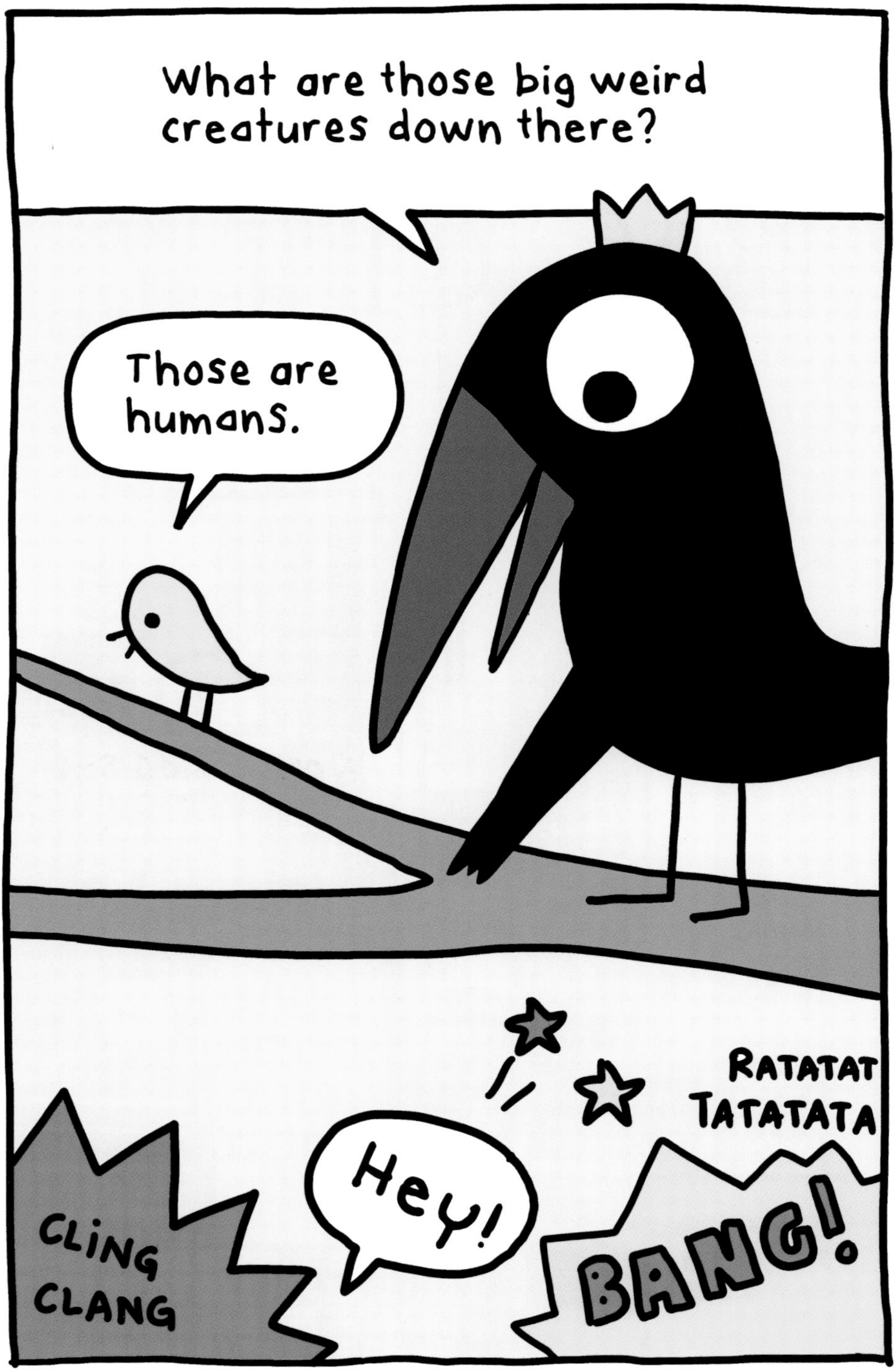
What are those big weird creatures down there?
Those are humans.
CLING CLANG
Hey!
RATATAT TATATATA
BANG!

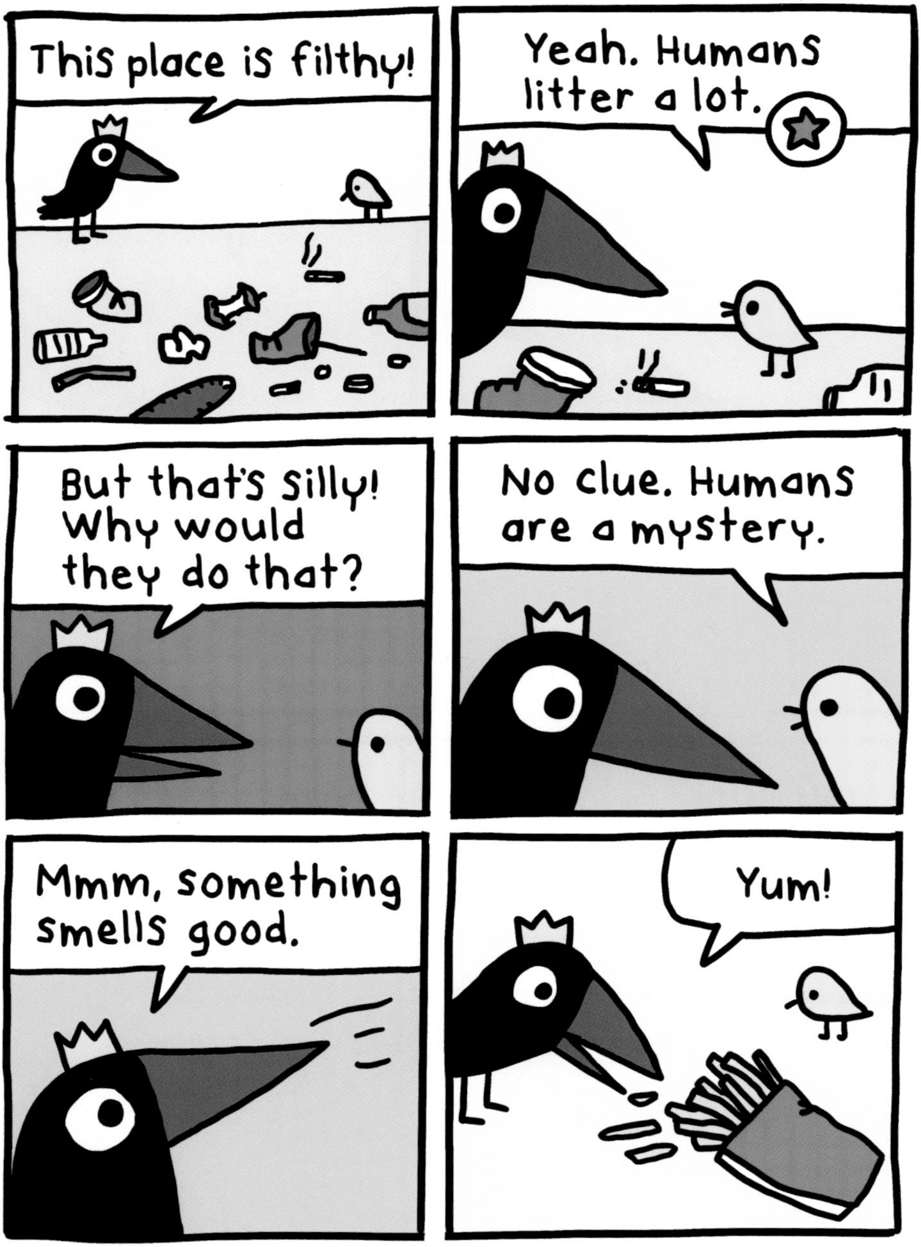
This place is filthy!
Yeah. Humans litter a lot.
But that's silly! Why would they do that?
No clue. Humans are a mystery.
Mmm, something smells good.
Yum!

★ Humans do litter a lot. (Sigh.)

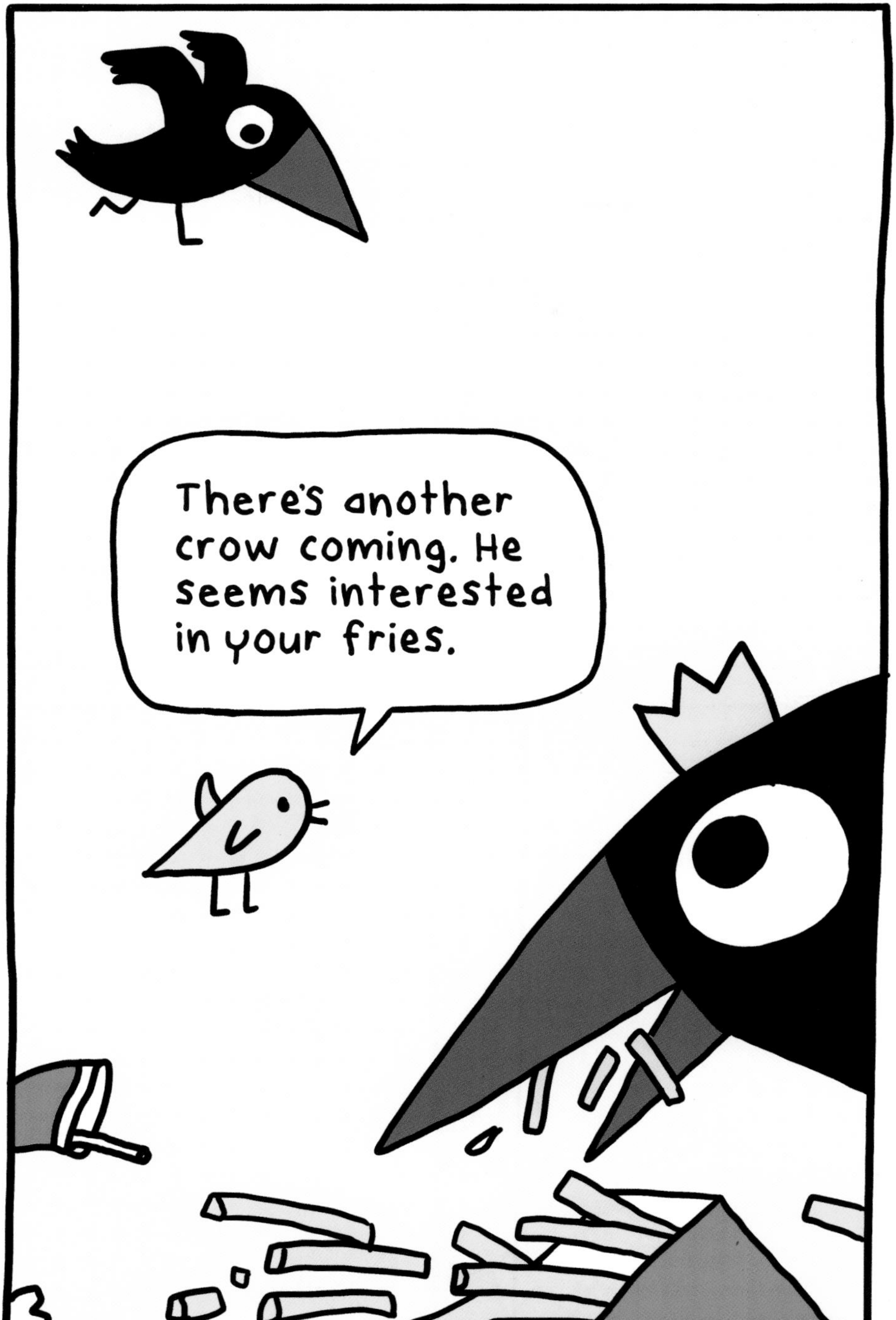
There's another crow coming. He seems interested in your fries.

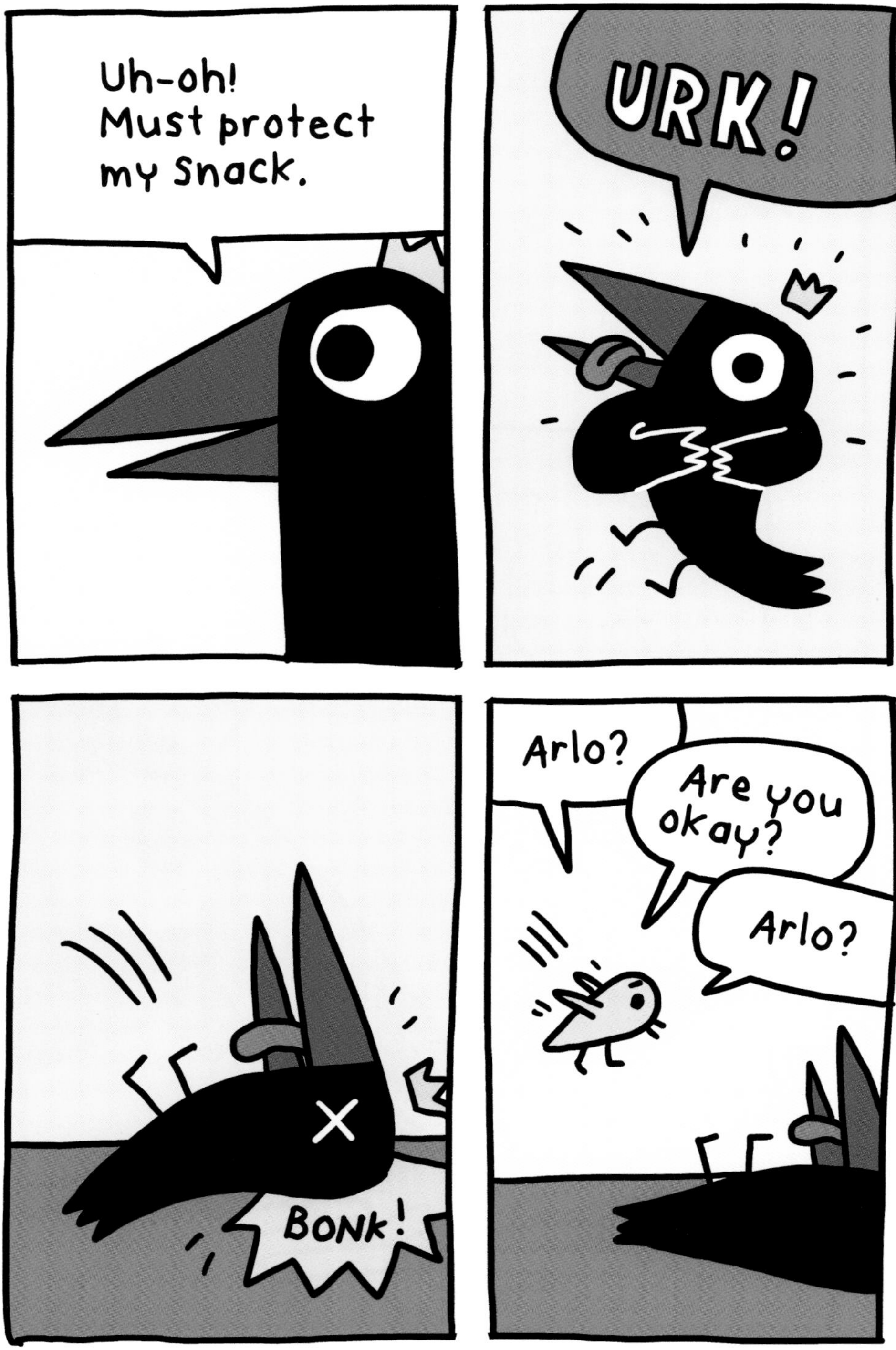
Uh-oh!
Must protect
my snack.
URK!
BONK!
Arlo?
Are you
okay?
Arlo?

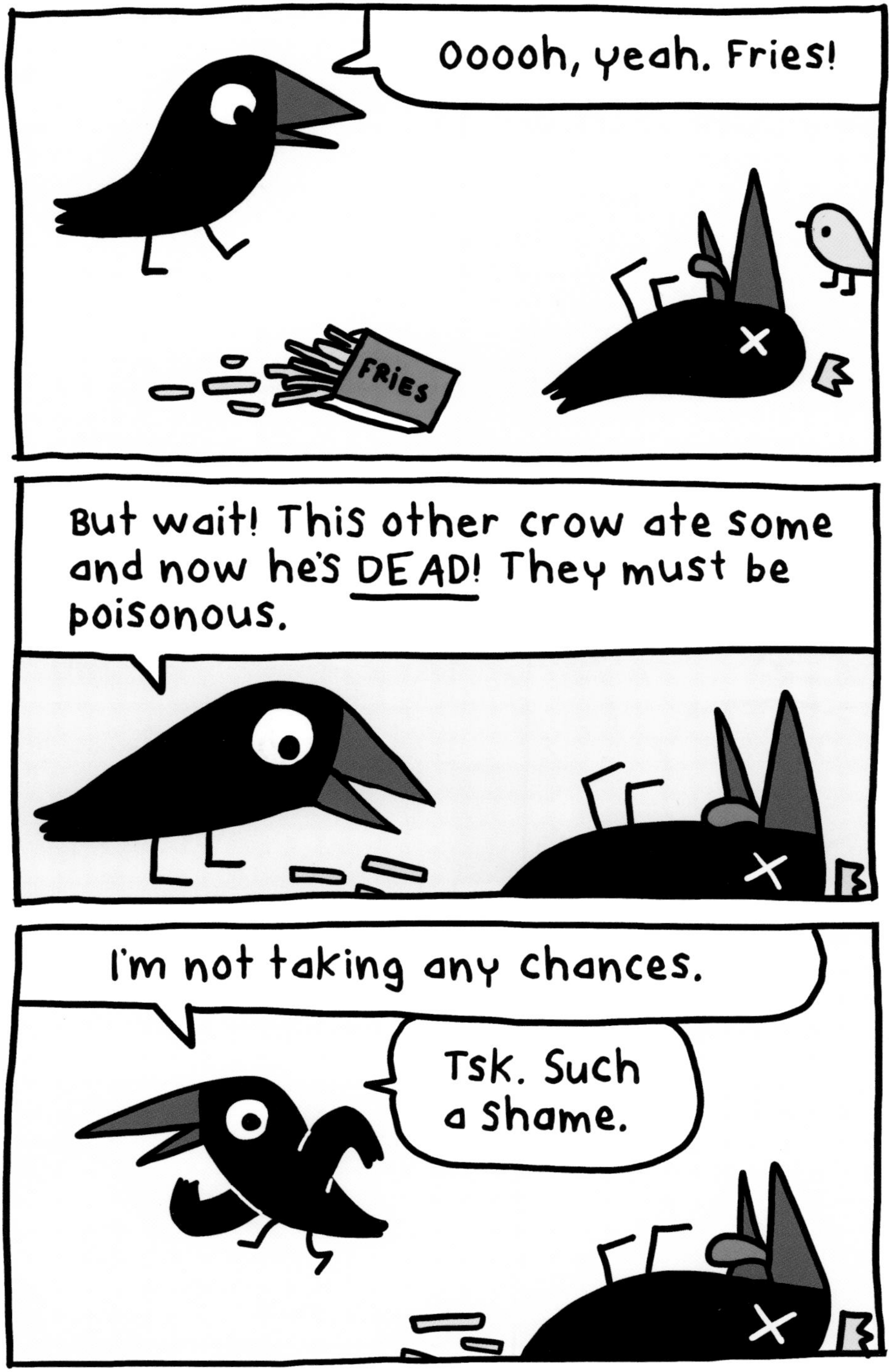
Ooooh, yeah. Fries!
FRIES
But wait! This other crow ate some and now he's DEAD! They must be poisonous.
I'm not taking any chances.
Tsk. Such a shame.

Some crows have been seen playing dead to fool other crows and keep food for themselves.

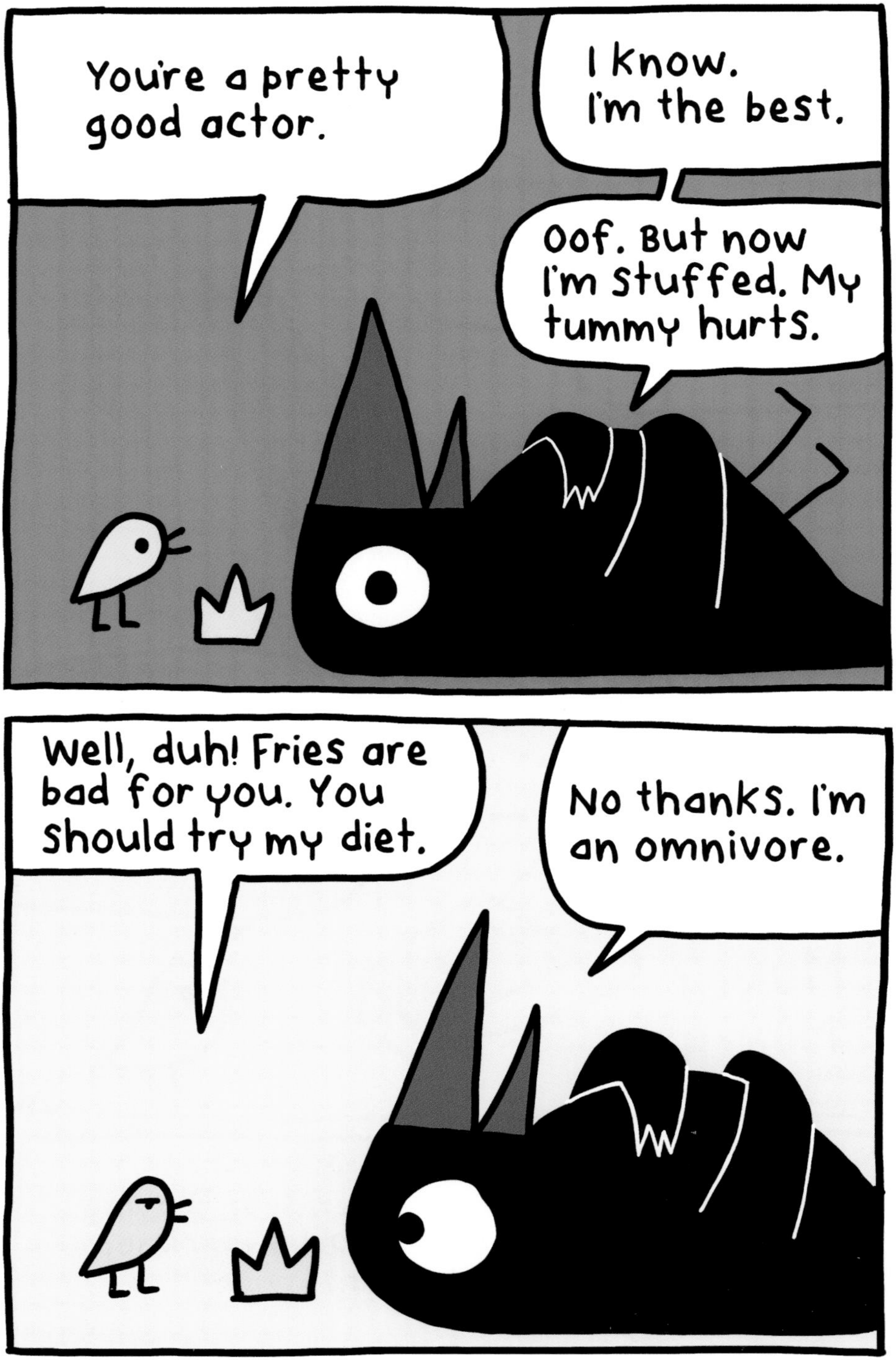
You're a pretty good actor.
I know. I'm the best.
Oof. But now I'm stuffed. My tummy hurts.
Well, duh! Fries are bad for you. You should try my diet.
No thanks. I'm an omnivore.

 Crows eat many things: seeds, fruit, small mammals, frogs, bugs, lizards, worms, eggs, nuts, mollusks, human food scraps . . . and yes, trash.

Crows can be taught tricks!
A French theme park trained
a team of crows to pick up trash.

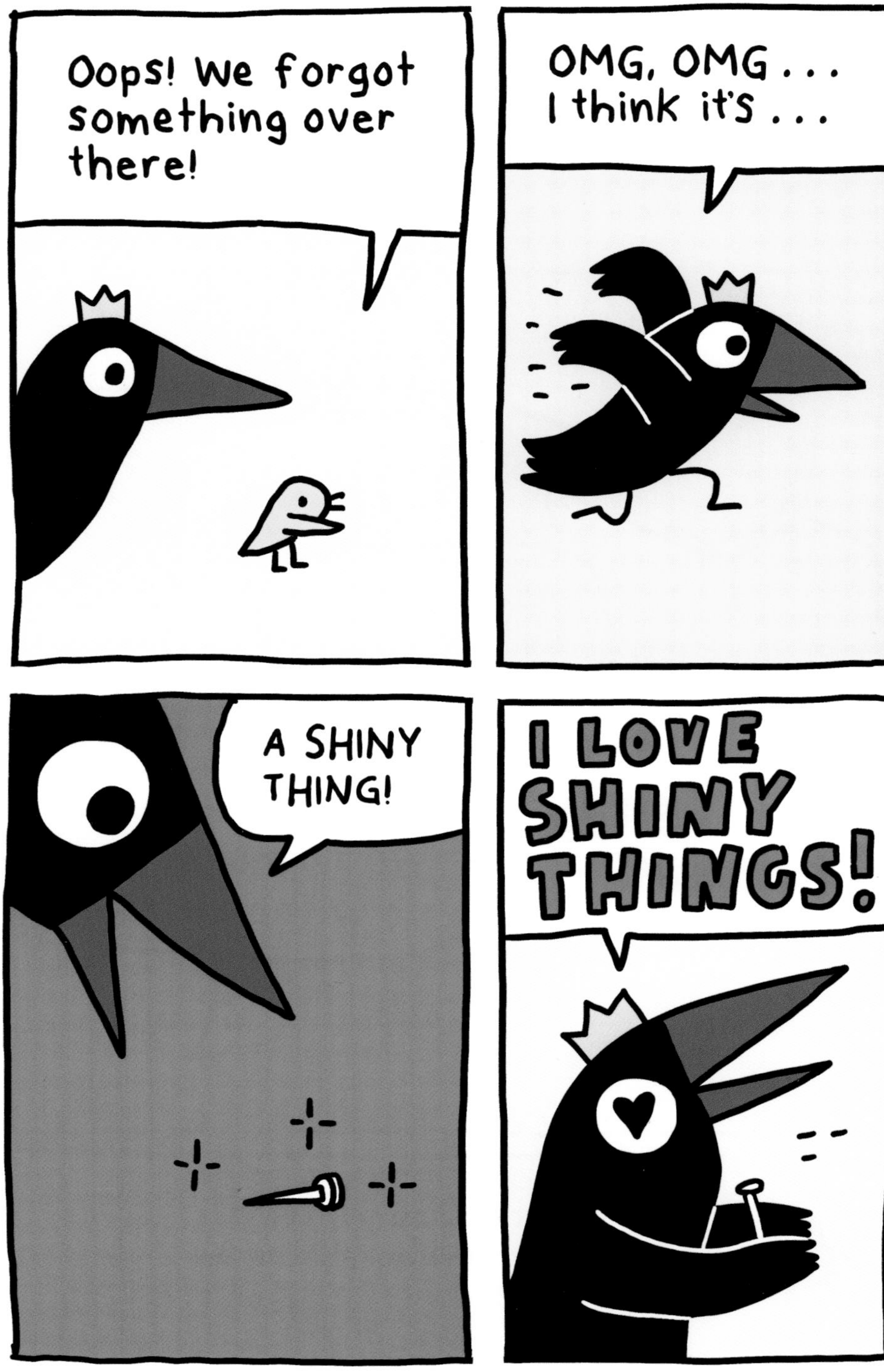
Oops! We forgot something over there!
OMG, OMG . . . I think it's . . .
A SHINY THING!
I LOVE SHINY THINGS!

Crows have a reputation for liking and collecting shiny objects.

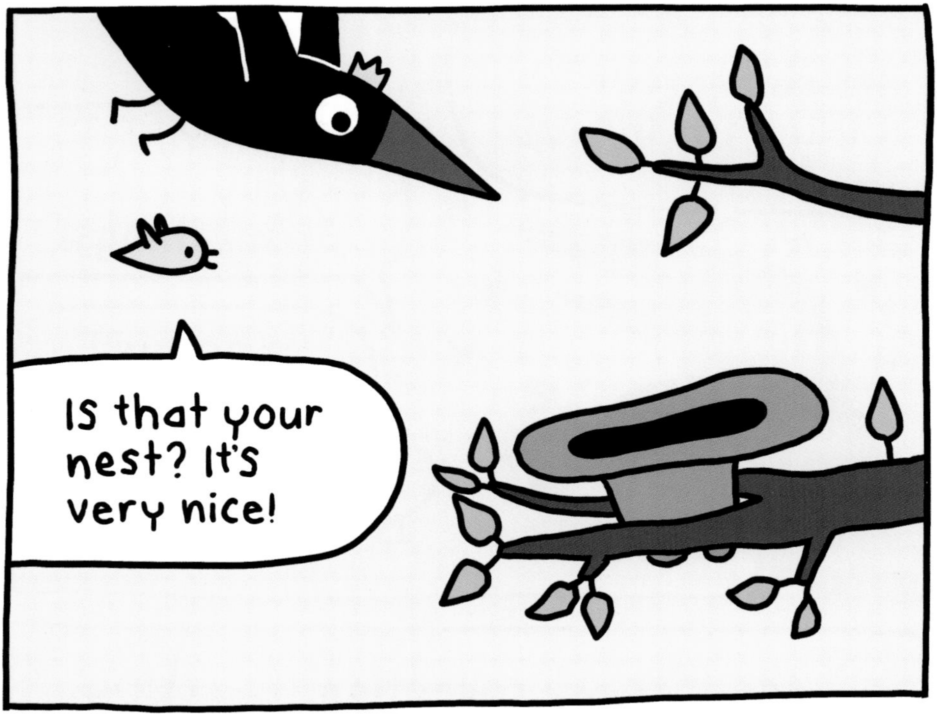
Is that your nest? It's very nice!

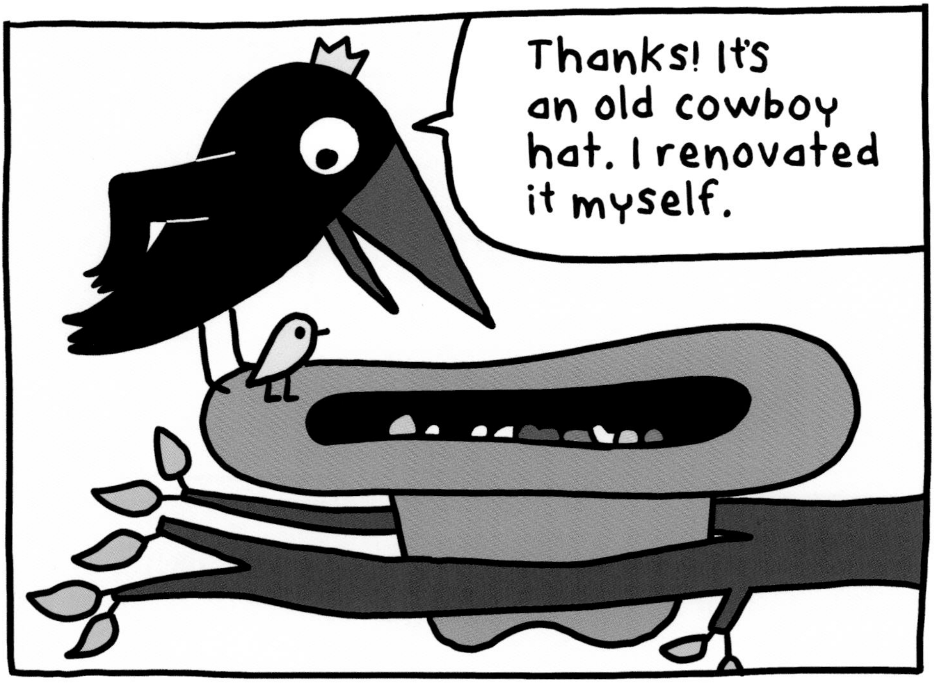
Thanks! It's an old cowboy hat. I renovated it myself.

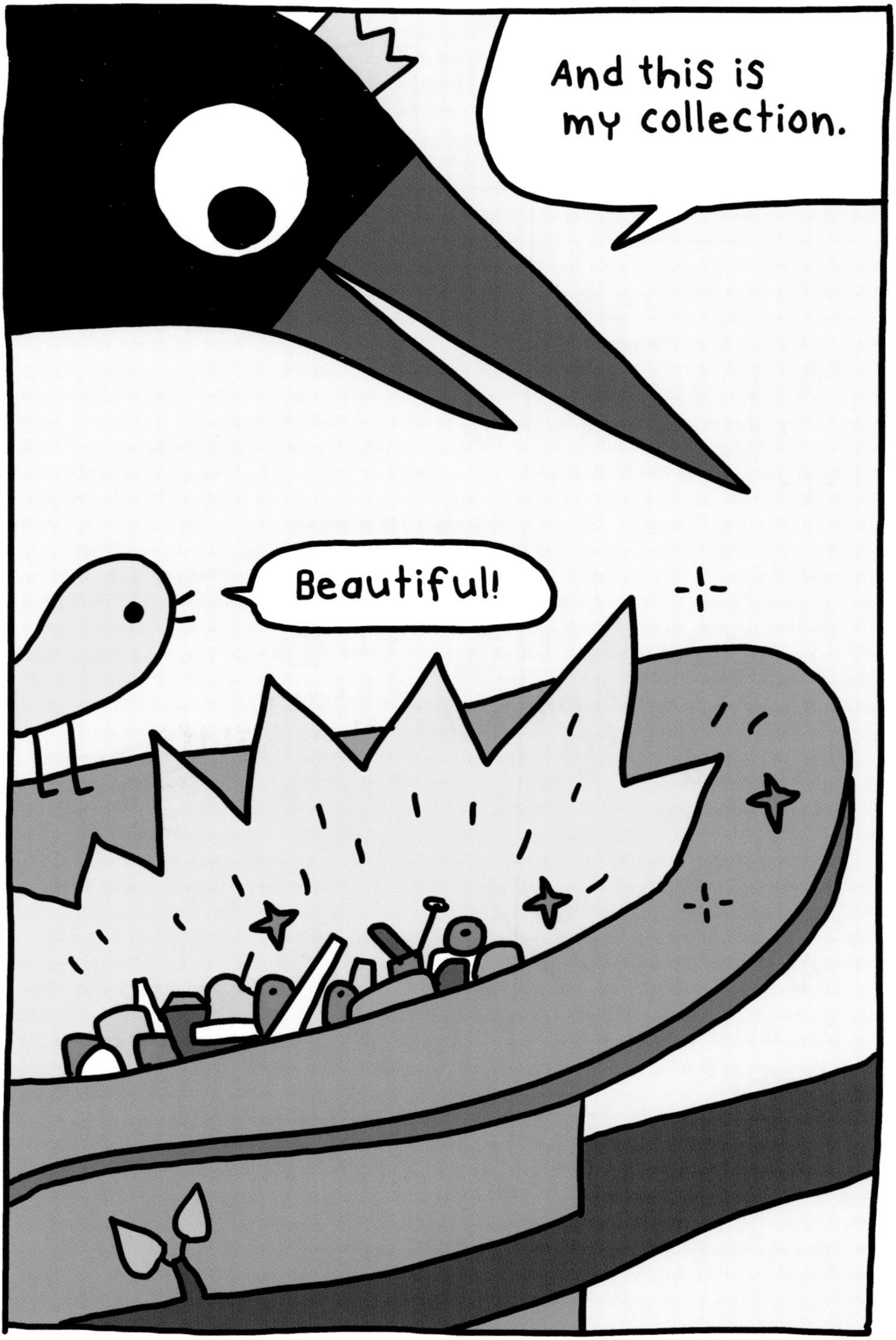
And this is my collection.
Beautiful!

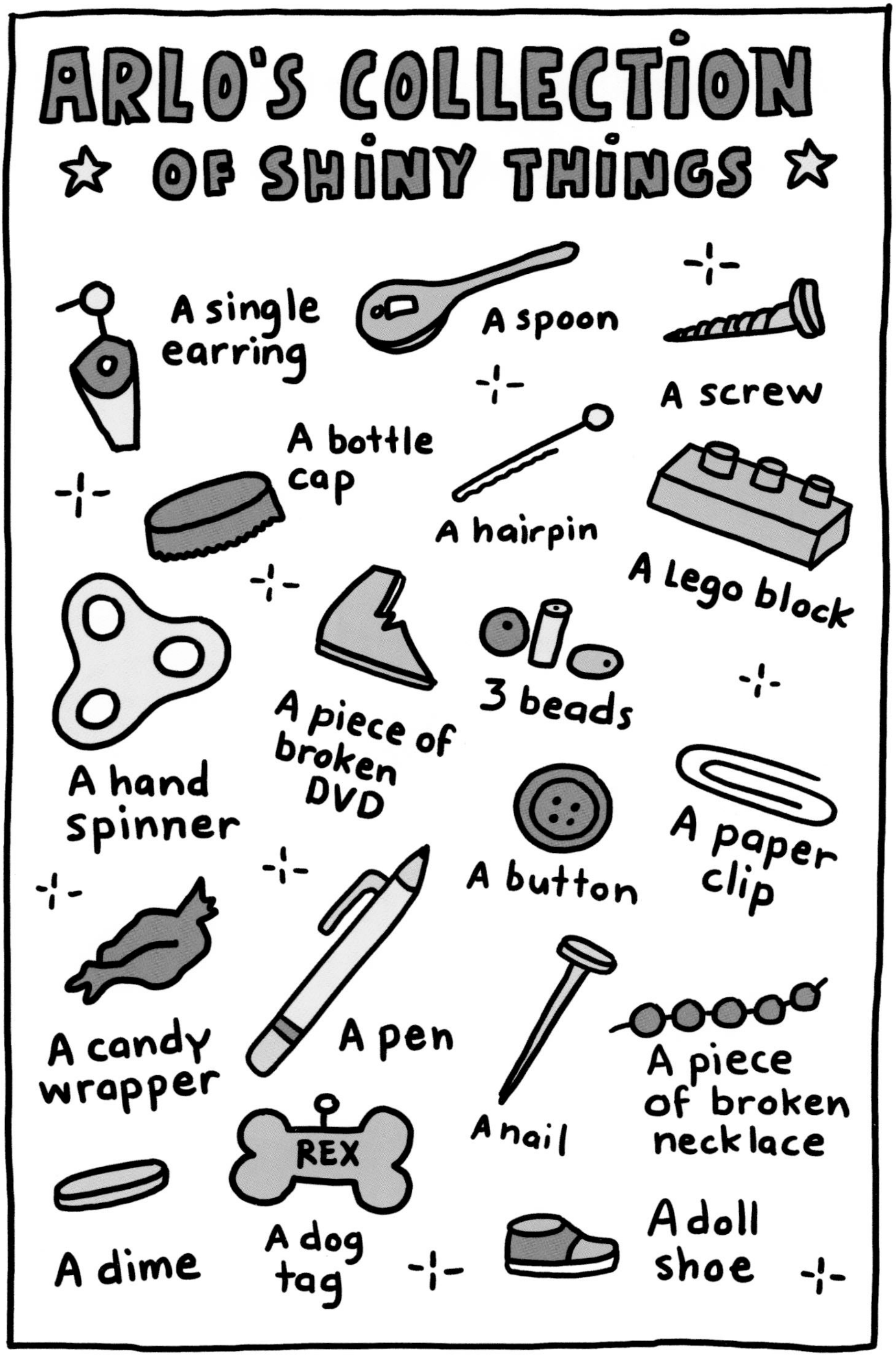
ARLO'S COLLECTION
OF SHINY THINGS
A single earring
A spoon
A screw
A bottle cap
A hairpin
A Lego block
A hand spinner
A piece of broken DVD
3 beads
A button
A paper clip
A candy wrapper
A pen
A nail
A piece of broken necklace
REX
A dime
A dog tag
A doll shoe

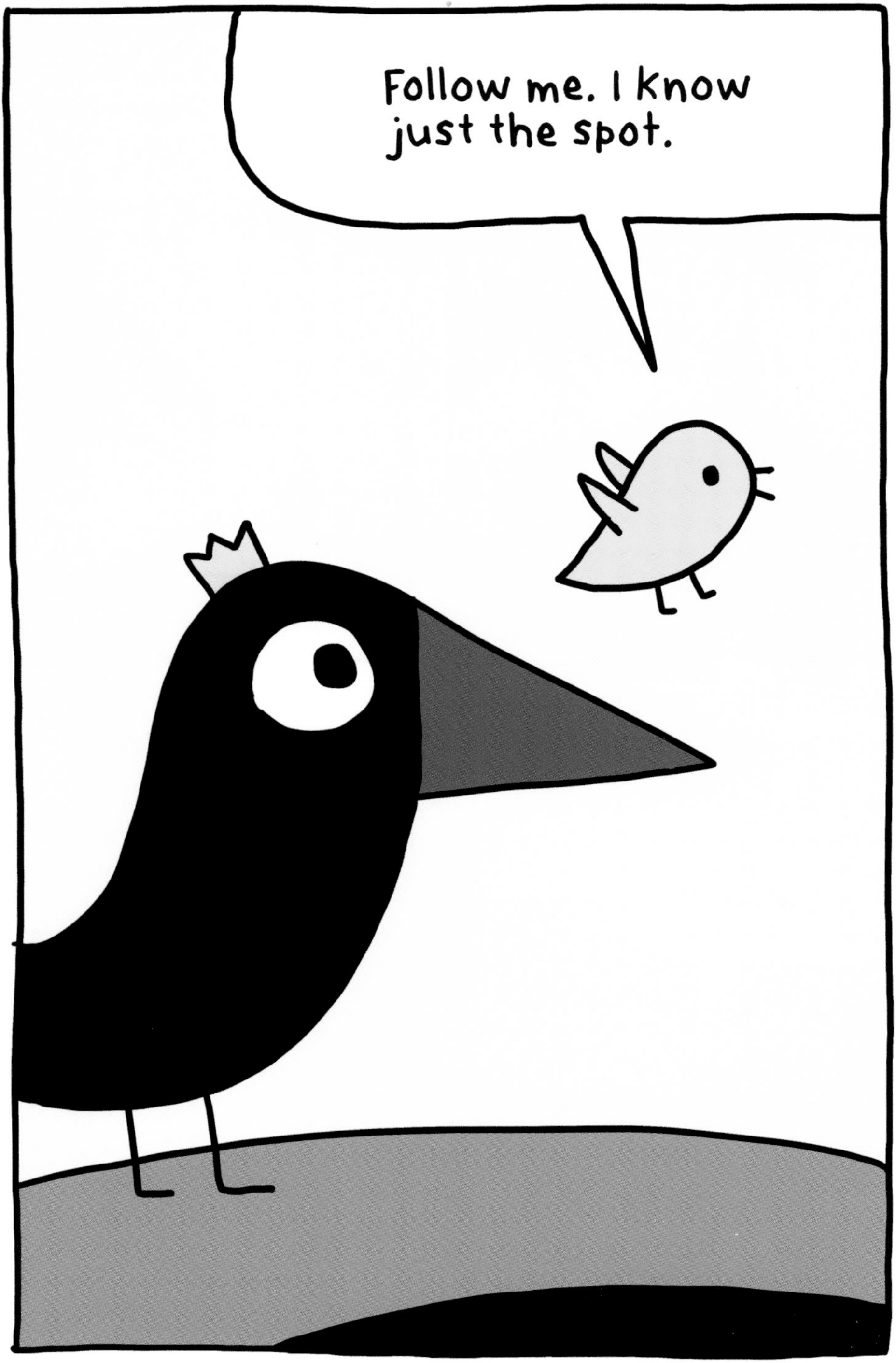
Follow me. I know just the spot.

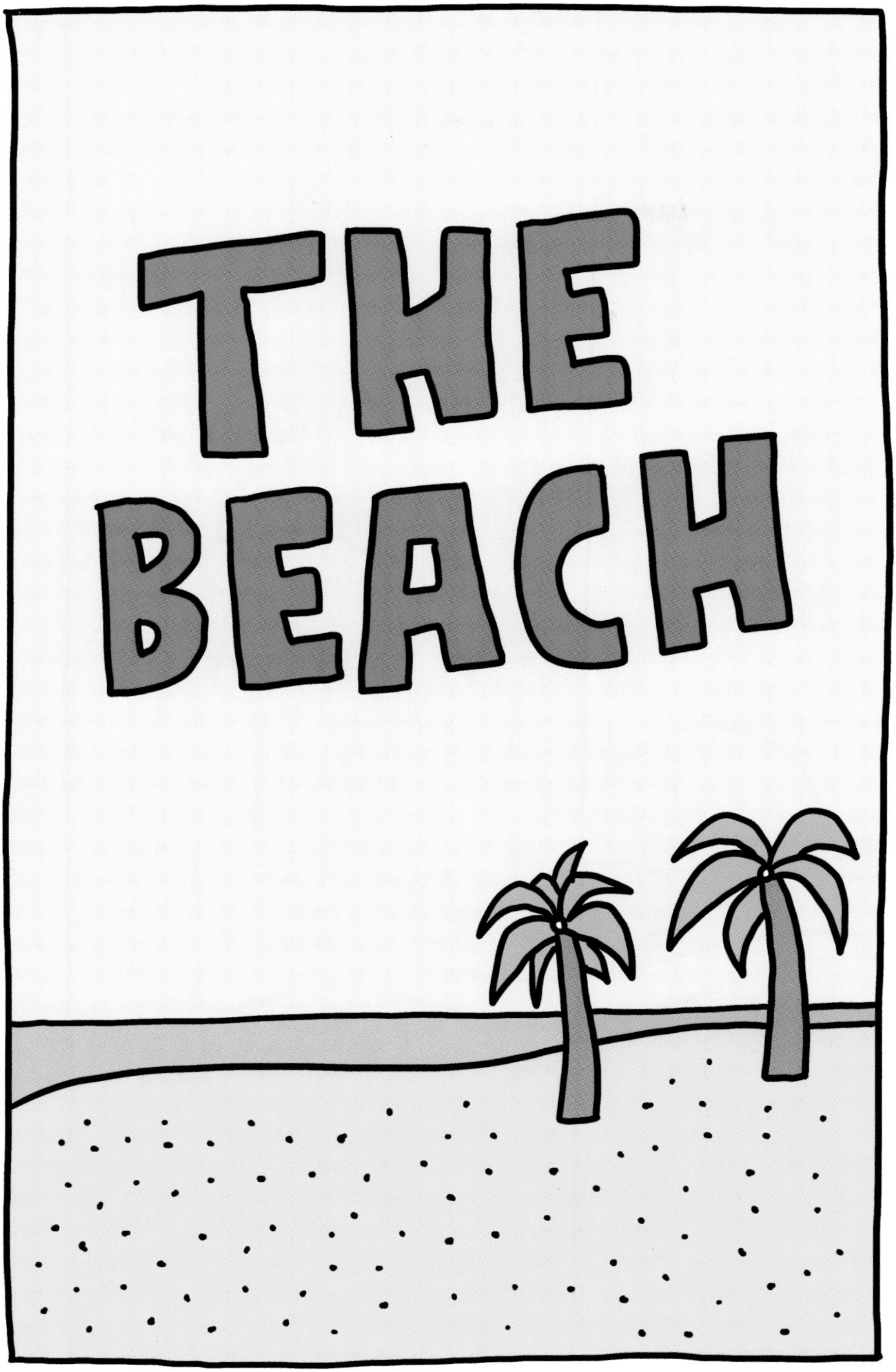
THE
BEACH

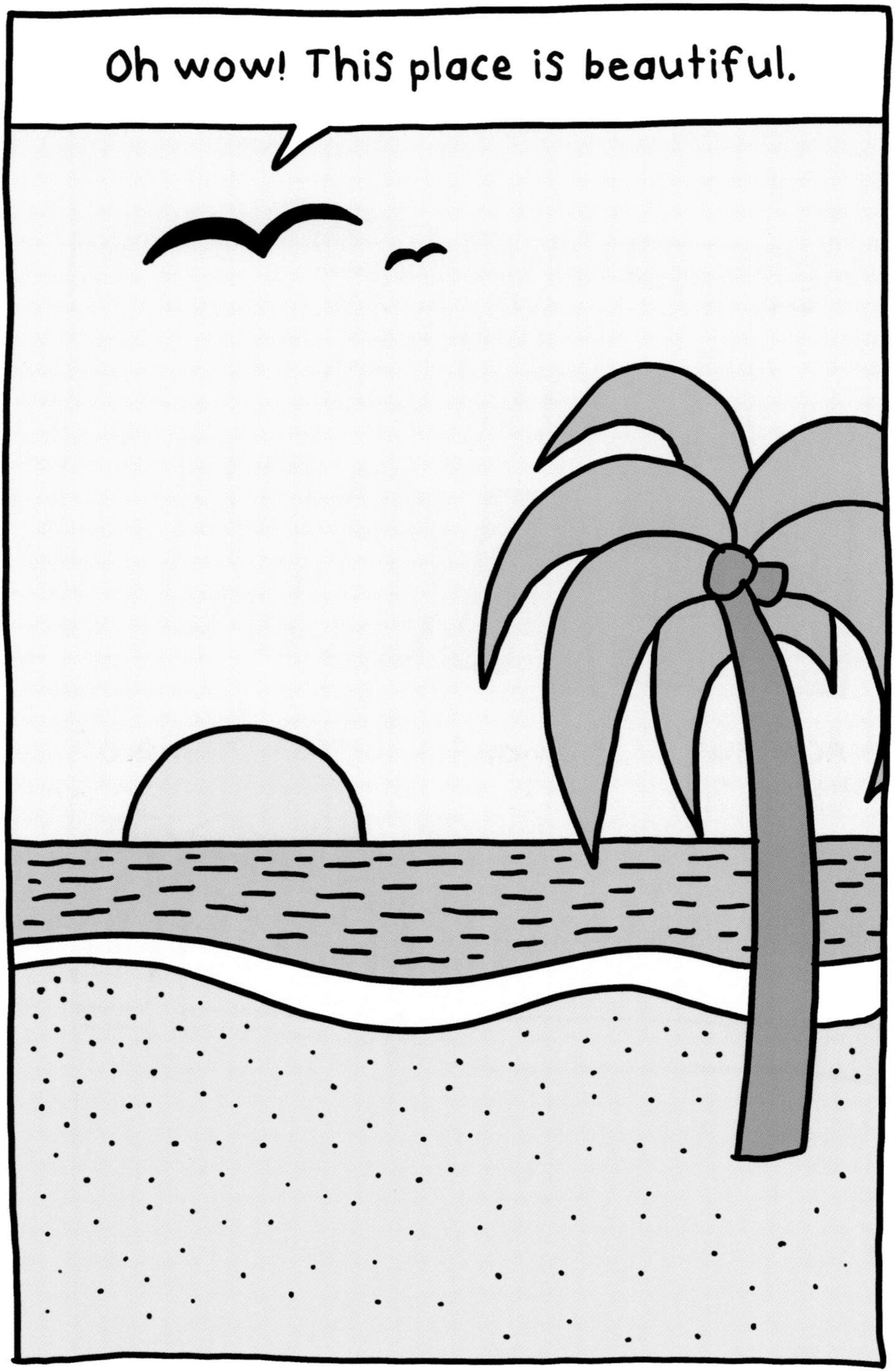
Oh wow! This place is beautiful.

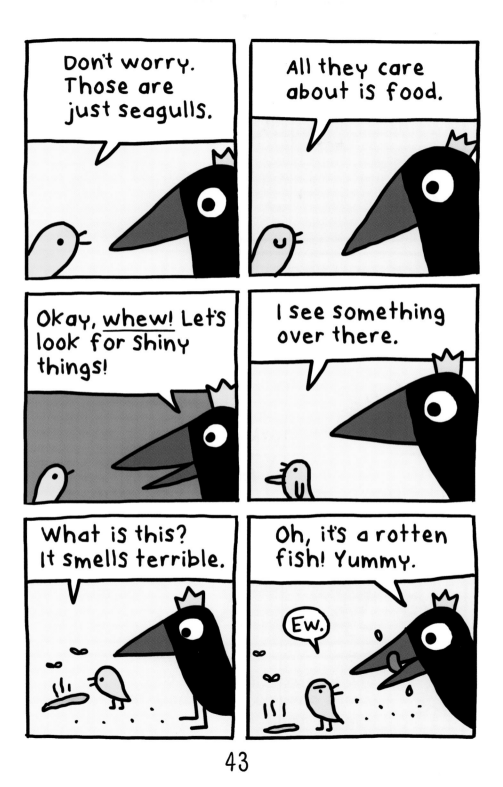

43

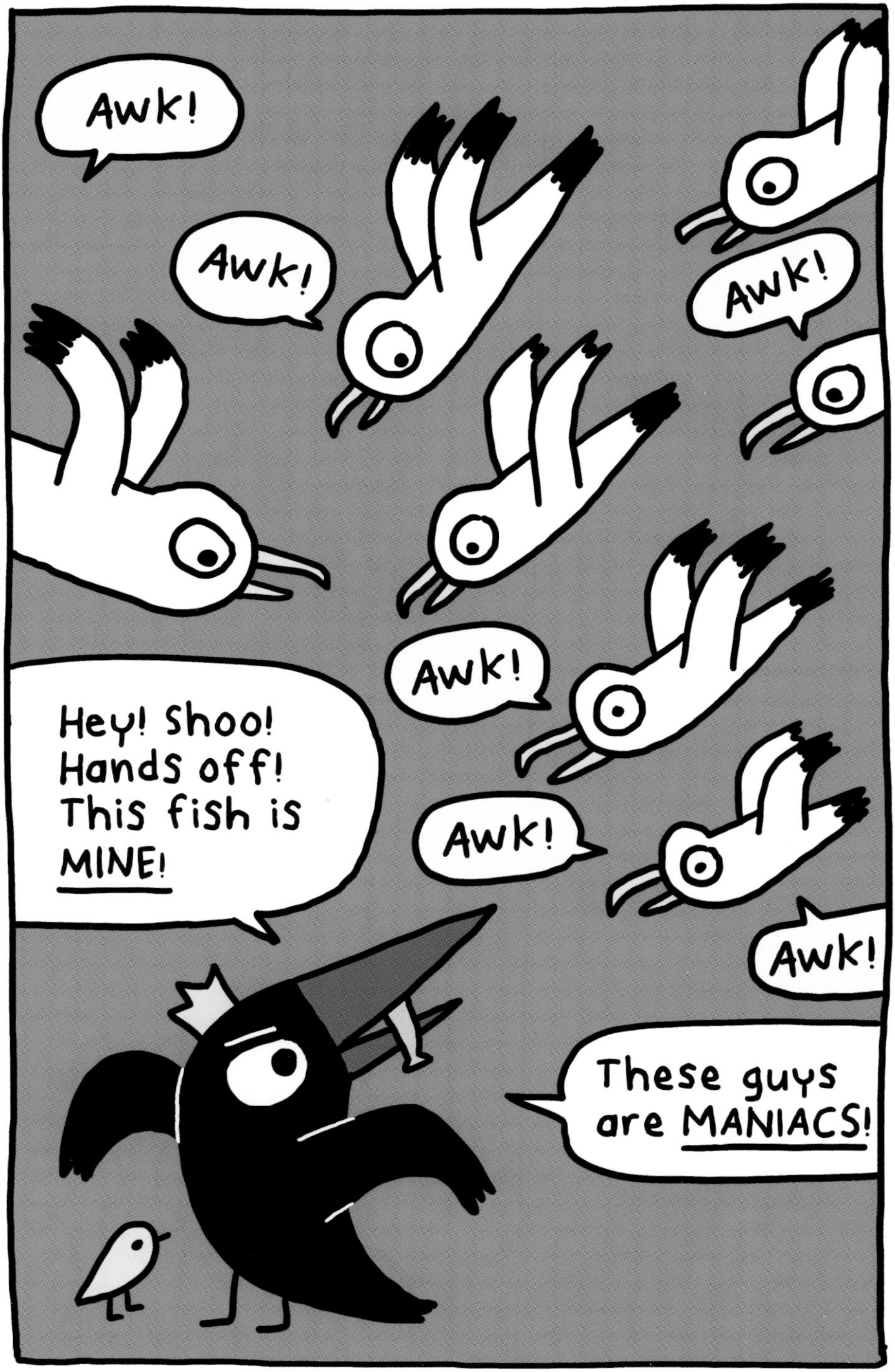
AWK!
AWK!
AWK!
AWK!
Hey! Shoo! Hands off! This fish is MINE!
AWK!
AWK!
These guys are MANIACS!

46

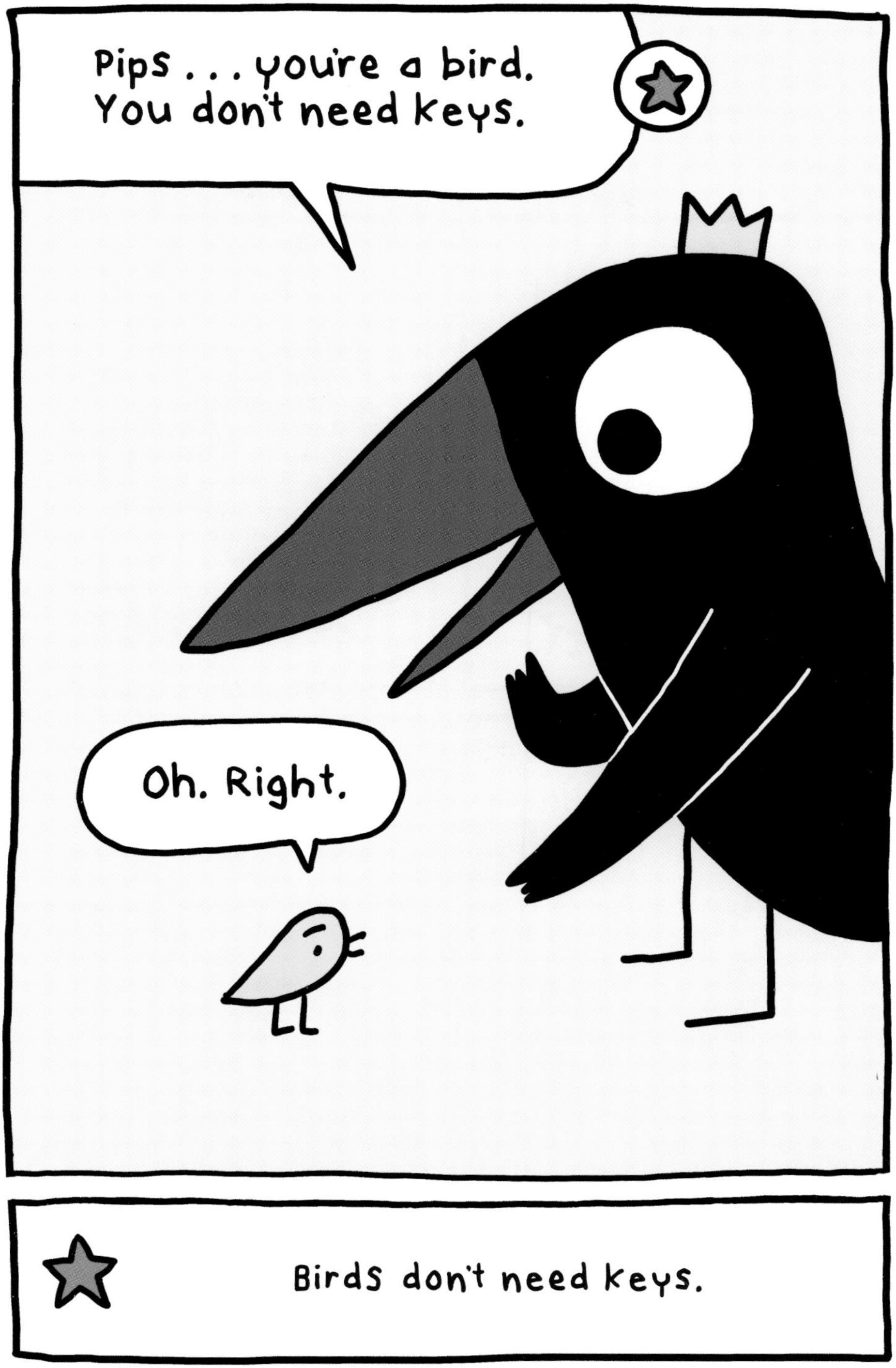
Pips . . . you're a bird. You don't need keys.
Oh. Right.
Birds don't need keys.

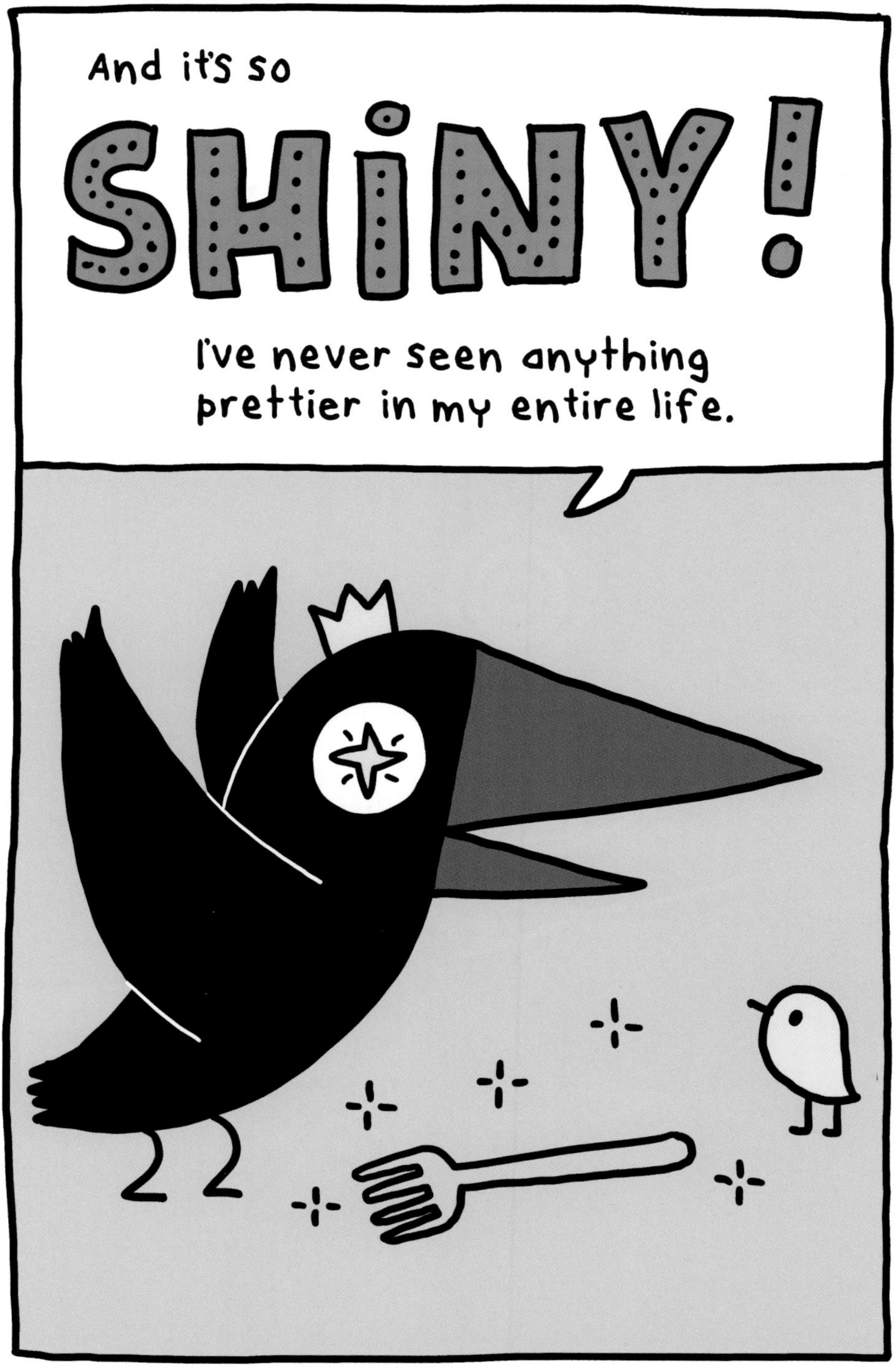
And it's so
SHiNY!
I've never seen anything prettier in my entire life.

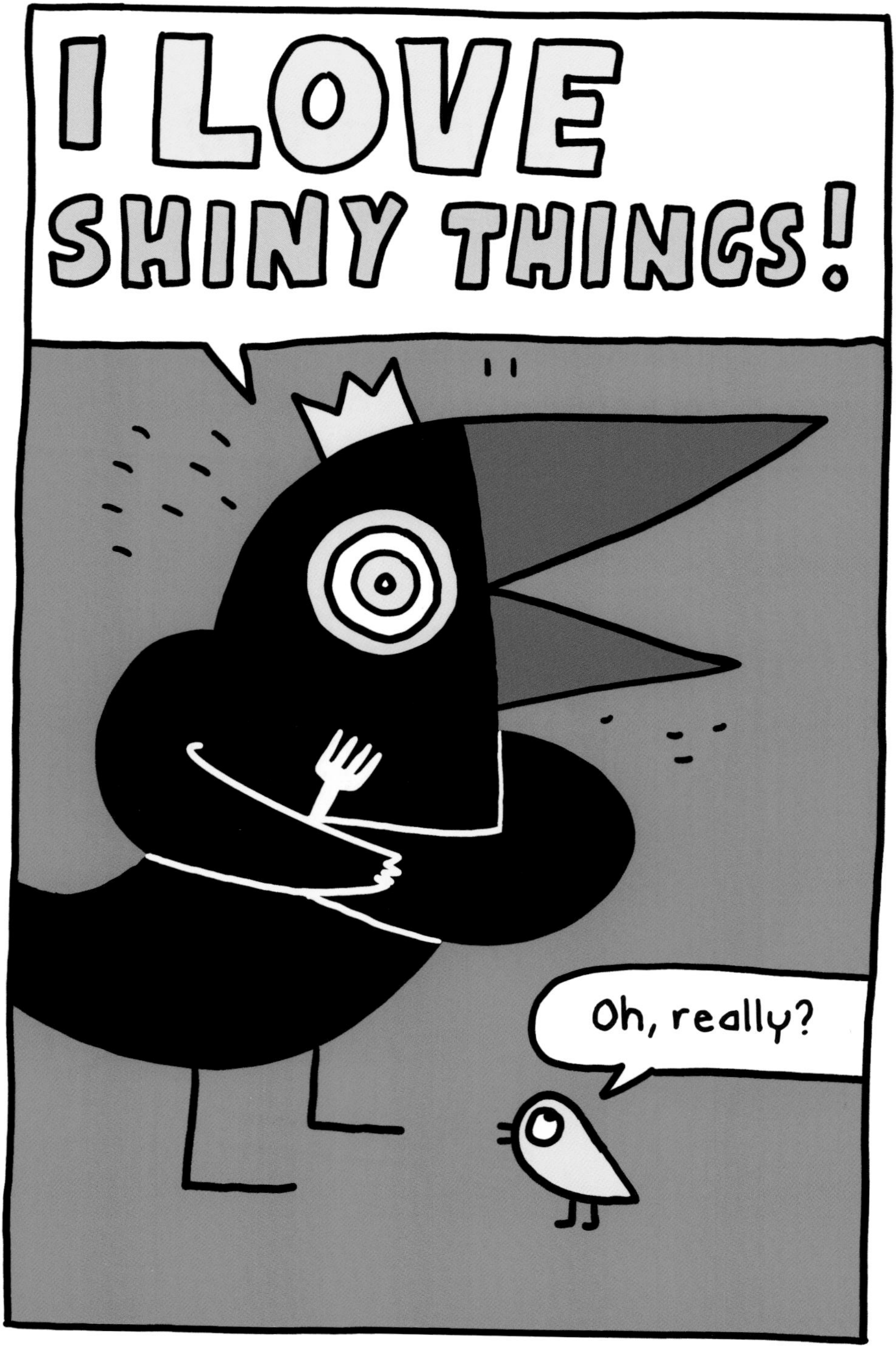
I LOVE SHINY THINGS!
Oh, really?

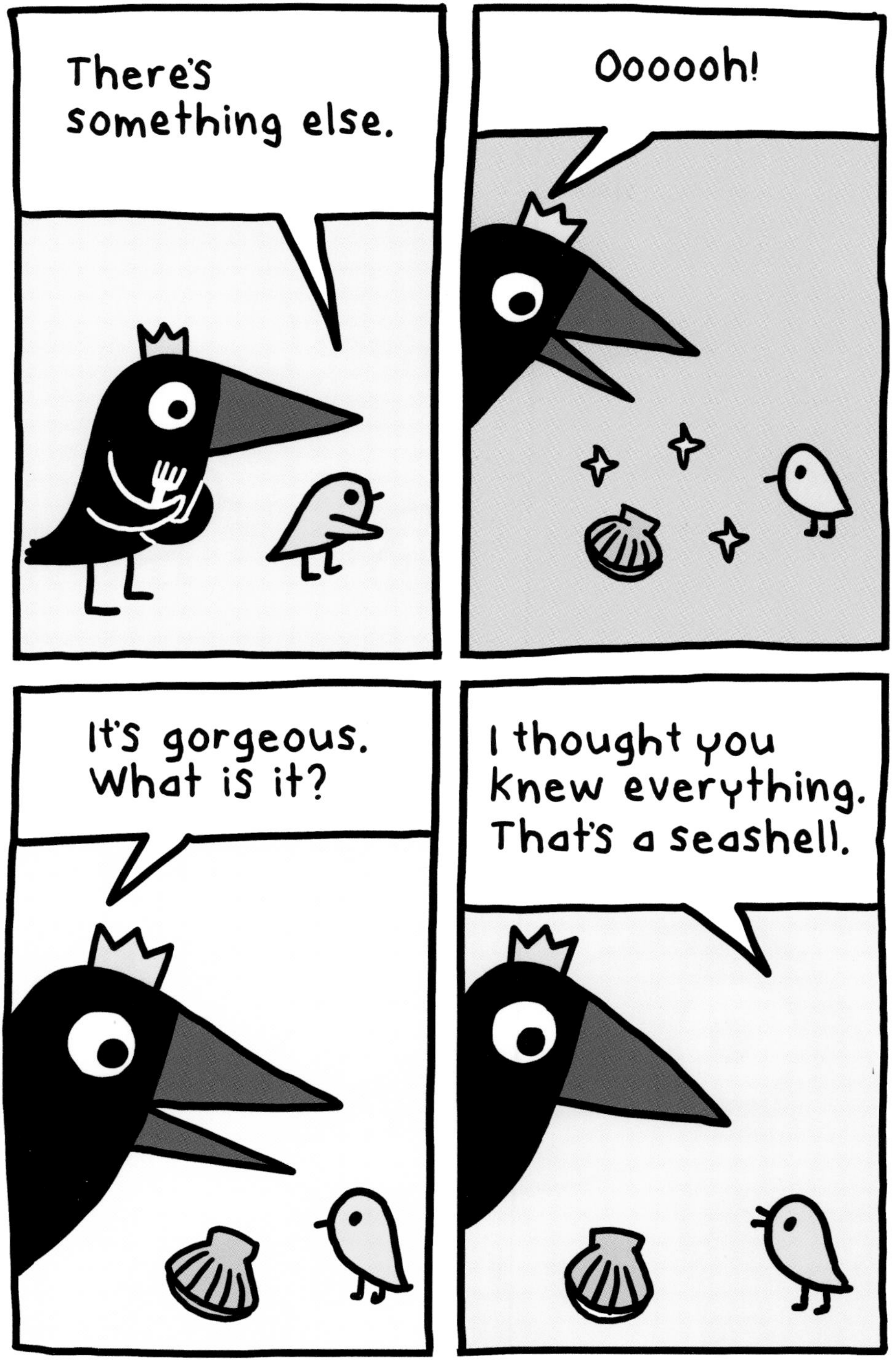
There's something else.
Oooooh!
It's gorgeous. What is it?
I thought you knew everything. That's a seashell.

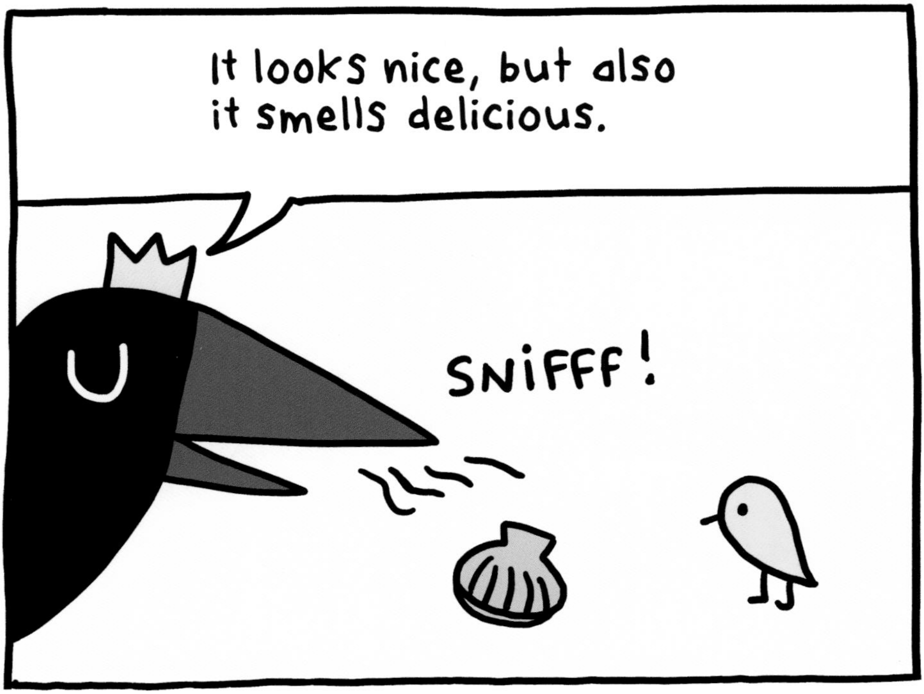
It looks nice, but also it smells delicious.
SNIFFF!

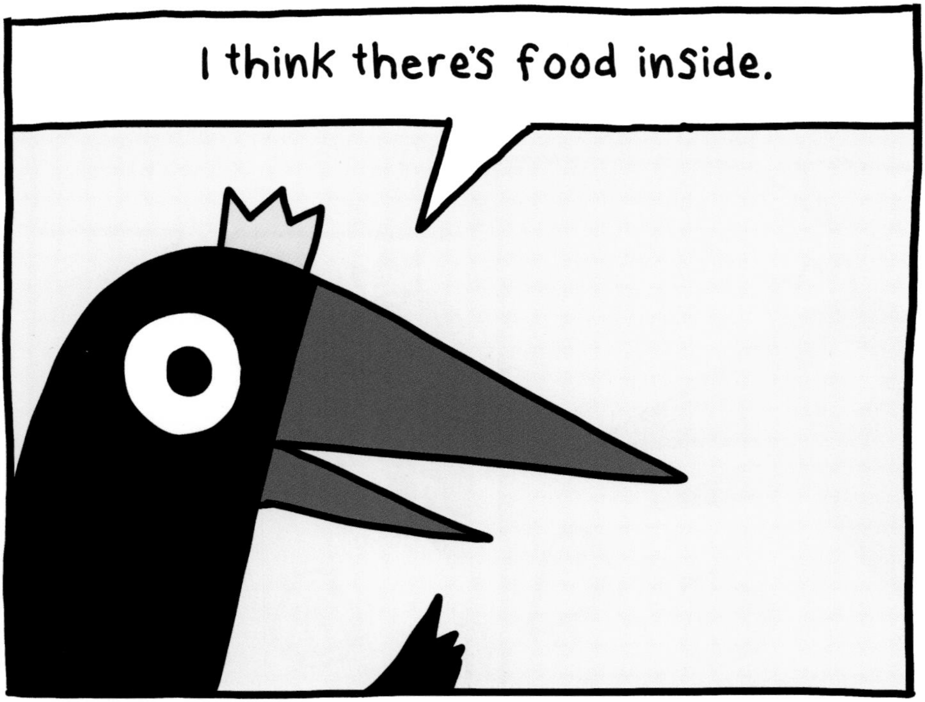
I think there's food inside.

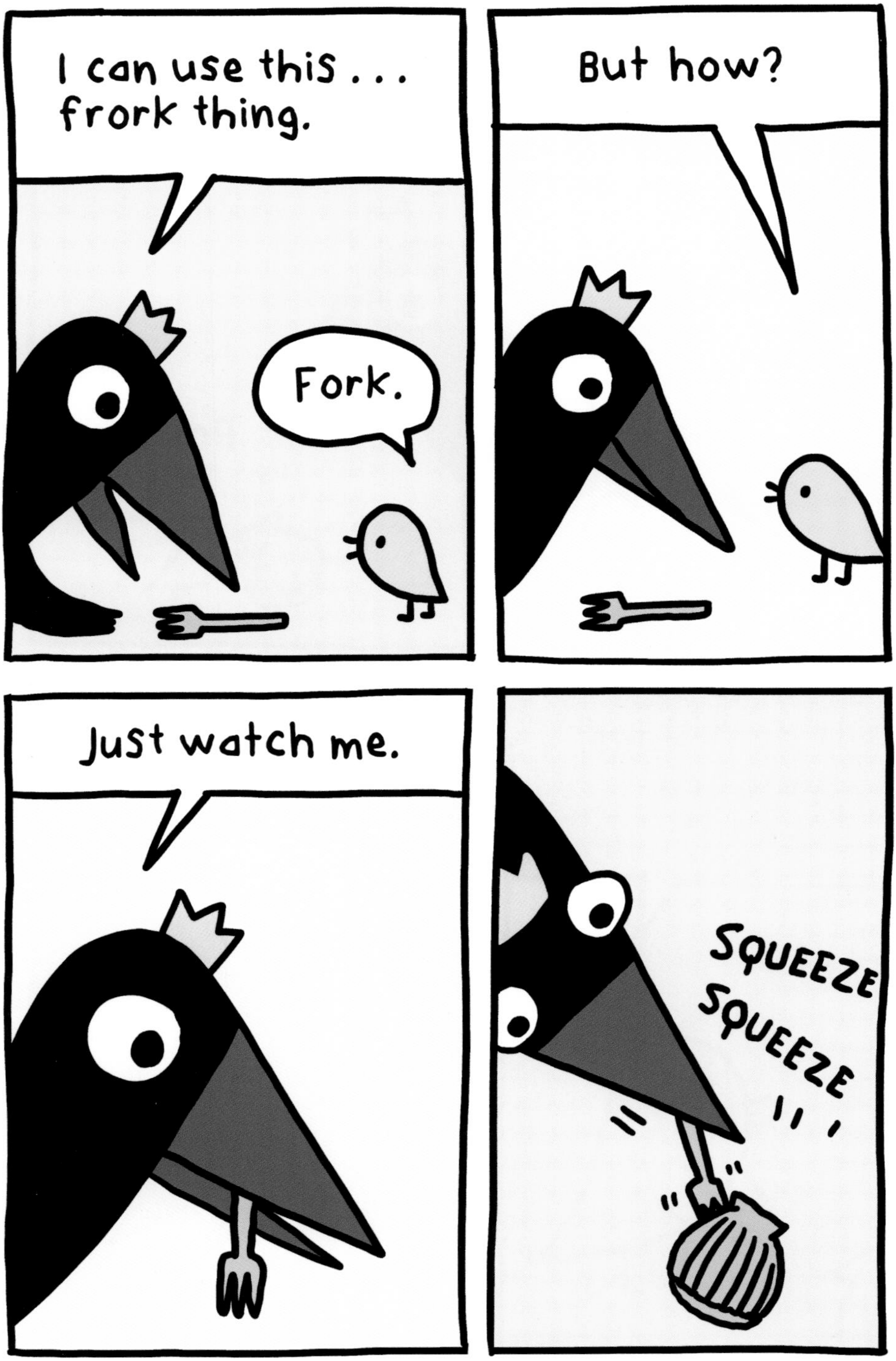
I can use this . . . frork thing.
Fork.
But how?
Just watch me.
SQUEEZE
SQUEEZE

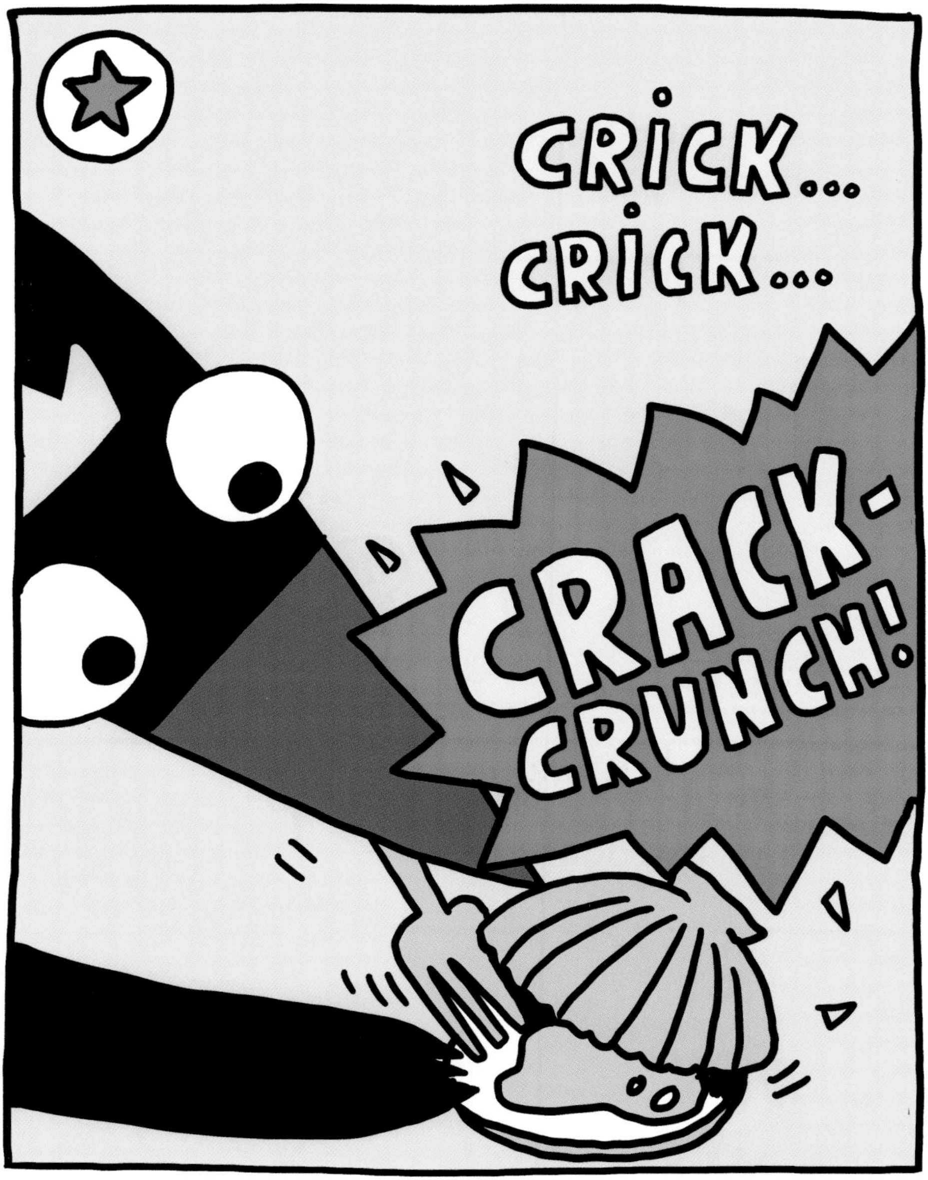
CRICK...
CRICK...
CRACK-
CRUNCH!

★ Crows can craft and use tools to access hard-to-reach food.

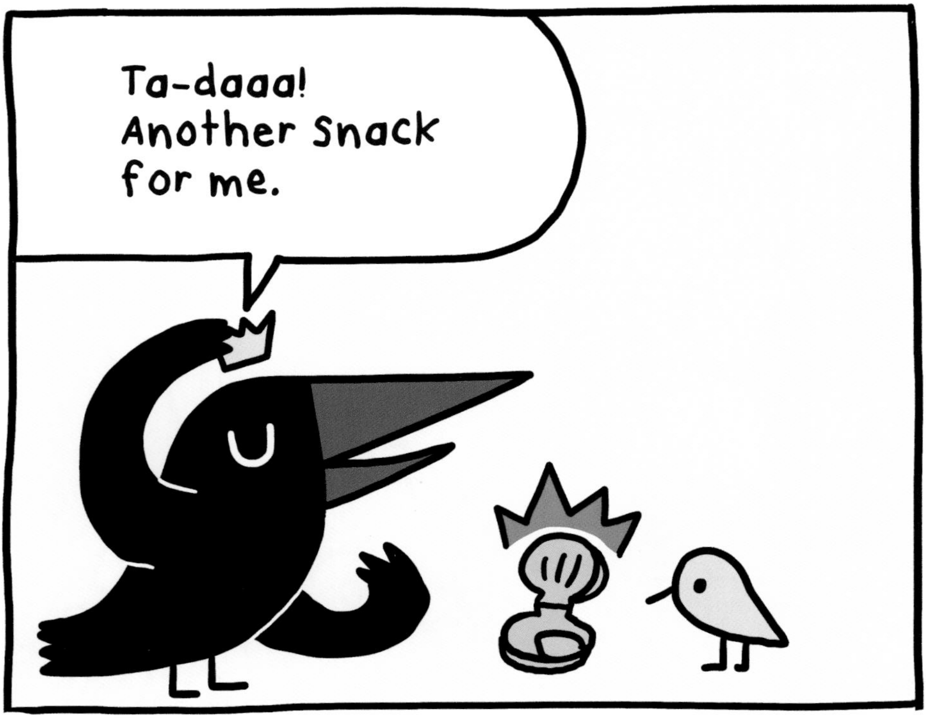
Ta-daaa! Another snack for me.

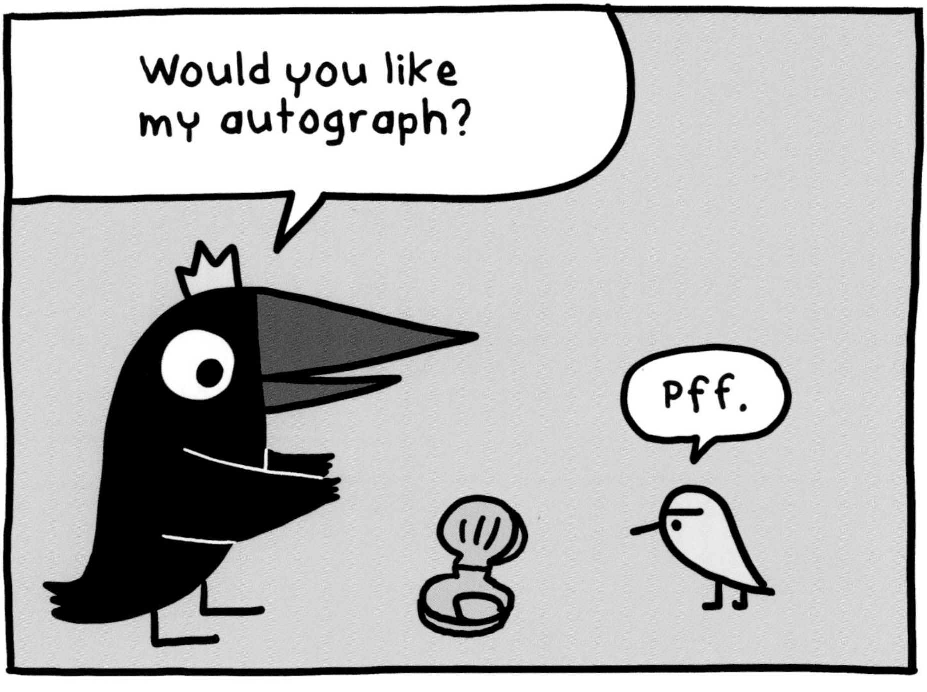
Would you like my autograph?
Pff.

STAY TUNED FOR
MORE ADVENTURES OF . . .